In the early 1850s eve[...]
River has potential for [...]
for drays to bring sto[...]
sheds packed with woo[...]
market.

The South Australian government offers a cash reward for the captains of the first two steam-powered vessels to not only arrive at the Murray, but travel upstream to the junction with the Darling.

Two men answer the call. The first is William Randell, from Gumeracha. William and his brothers build their fifty-five foot *Mary Ann* in an Adelaide Hills sawpit, then assemble it on the banks of the Murray, installing a small beam-type steam engine made by a local engineer of German descent.

The second man to throw his hat into the ring is Captain Cadell, a sea captain of long experience and a budding entrepreneur with grandiose designs. With the help of wealthy investors, Cadell has his 105 foot *Lady Augusta* built in a Darling Harbour shipyard, with twin state-of-the-art horizontal steam engines, and accommodation for thirty.

Cadell and Randell would both like to be remembered as the founders of Murray River navigation. Both are ambitious and highly skilled in their own way. This is the story of what happens when they pit their skills against each other, and against one of the mightiest rivers on earth.

Also by Greg Barron

HarperCollins Publishers Australia
Rotten Gods
Savage Tide
Lethal Sky
Voodoo Dawn (short fiction)

Stories of Oz Publishing
The Hammer of Ramenskoye (short fiction)
Camp Leichhardt
Galloping Jones and Other True Stories from
Australia's History
Whistler's Bones
Red Jack and the Ragged Thirteen
Outlaw: The Story of Joe Flick
The Time of Thunder
The Last Days of Dom Sebastian
Will Jones and the Dead Man's Letter (novella)

Beyond the Big Bend

Greg Barron

STORIES OF
OZ

First edition published 2022
by **Stories of Oz** Publishing
PO Box K57
Haymarket NSW 1240

ABN: 0920230558
facebook.com/storiesofoz
ozbookstore.com

The right of Greg Barron to be identified as the author
of this work has been asserted by him in accordance
with the Copyright Amendment (Moral Rights) Act
2000

© 2022 Greg Barron
ISBN: 9780645351132
Cover Design: James Barron
Technical reader: Frank Tucker
Typeset in 12/17-point Garamond
Printed and bound in Australia by IngramSpark

To the men and women of the Murray River, from
the Dreamtime to today.

RIVER MURRAY

Minne...g...
Yongdulla to Bhending to Rusell Creek
Panguruptum

Chittour

Pomanda

To Port Phillip

Extensive Plains
Tooant
Maroungwa
Lagoon

DESERT

Extensive Flats
Swamp

Grass rising in...
Dead up Salt Lagoon

Mylunga

from Adelaide

Saltwater Scrub
Samphry Scrub

Point Malcolm
Pomuda
Poolhowa

Undulating Grassy Country
Thickly Wooded with Casuarina
and Banksia and Pine

Mineral Flat

LAKE ALBERT

Waterways
Water bottled
Sand

Grass rising in...

River Meechi or Bremer

Rich Plains
Thickly timbered with Gum

Tooant
Ist Stuart

P... Lake Kundon?
Black...

Undulating Grassy Country
Tightly Wooded Casuarina

Rich Mineral Flat

Numerous Salt Lagoons

Undulating Wooded Grassy Country

COORONG

LAKE ALEXANDRINA

Track

Sandy Soil
stale Tippity Creek

Sandy Soil
Casuarina

Salt Lagoon

Finniss

from Adelaide River

HINDMARSH I.

from Adelaide Via Willunga

Currency Creek

Hindoo Channel

Mundoo I.

ENCOUNTER BAY

Pullins I?
Willungepool

Ye Granite I?
Va Seal Rock
Victor Harbour
Rosetta Harbour
Rosetta Head

from Adelaide

R. Hindmarsh

Soundings in feet at Low Water.

THE
MURRAY
RIVER

FROM THE MOUTH TO MOAMA
APPROX 1070 RIVER MILES (1700 KM)

PROLOGUE

The Prize

THE MURRAY RIVER, called Dhungala by the Yorta Yorta, and Millewa by the Ngarrindjeri, was once as wild and free as the land over which it flowed. In those days before reservoirs and locks it ran unbroken and unhindered from the Snowy Mountains, meeting other important rivers – the Ovens, Goulburn and Loddon – gathering volume with each junction. It wound through the red gum forests of the Barmah Choke then collected the Murrumbidgee. It ran serenely through vast reed beds near Swan Hill, until it met the Barka – the Darling, winding all the way down from Queensland. This combined river, the mighty Murray in its final form, flowed on into South Australia, around the Big Bend with its towering limestone cliffs, to Lake Alexandrina and a dangerous, shifting ocean bar.

In its natural flow, the Murray River had moods and seasons, rising in June from winter rain and snow-melt in the Snowy Mountains, spilling over her dry-season bed until October. From then on, through summer, the river shrank, a pattern broken only by monsoonal or cyclonic rains far up the Darling. These downpours spawned floods that spread out over the plains, idling downstream at a speed of a hundred miles a day.

Powerbrokers and colonial administrators had talked for years of how the river could become a transport artery like the Rhine, Mississippi, or the Nile. How bales of the world's best wool that took three months to cart from remote stations to the city by bullock dray, would travel by water in mere weeks.

In 1851, the South Australian legislature requested funds from the Lords' Treasurers in London to reward intrepid adventurers prepared to open the river trade. The sum of four thousand pounds was duly approved, and South Australian newspapers proclaimed that the government would pay half this amount to the owners of the *first and second iron steamers, of not less than forty horsepower, and not exceeding two feet of draught, that shall navigate from the Goolwa, at least as far as the junction of the Darling, a distance of some 490 miles.*

Scotsman Captain Francis Cadell, always alert to opportunities to increase his power and improve his finances, heard the call. An experienced mariner, having started as a midshipman at the age of fourteen, he was in South Australia as captain and owner of the clipper, *Queen of Sheba.* Already he was intimate with the governor, and he dined at the finest tables in Adelaide.

The other main player in this drama was less well-travelled but just as interesting. William Randell, at just twenty-nine years of age, was already deeply committed to building a paddle steamer for river trade – his family owned a flour mill at Gumeracha in the Adelaide Hills, and farmland at Noa No near Mannum. He dreamed of trading up the river in his own vessel.

Thus, partly by chance, and partly by design, in August 1853 two paddle steamers became rivals for the title of the first steam-powered vessel to navigate the Murray to Swan Hill.

William Randell's *Mary Ann* was home-made from pit-sawn river red gum logs in the Kenton Valley, Adelaide Hills, and assembled on the banks of the river at Noa No. The work was done by two bush carpenters and three brothers who had never seen such a vessel in their lives. Her seven-horsepower engine was made by a local engineer, and her boiler by the blacksmith at the family flour mill. When the *Mary Ann* set out to conquer the river she had a crew of five.

The *Lady Augusta* was constructed by some of Sydney's best shipwrights, in a Darling Harbour yard. At just under one hundred feet she was twice the length of the *Mary Ann* with many times the tonnage. She had twin twenty-horsepower steam engines, and had been built with no expense spared. She set off with forty on board, including the Governor of South Australia and his wife.

Given that the *Mary Ann* didn't meet the criteria set down by the South Australian government there is no certainty that William Randell cared much about the cash prize offered by the South Australian government. Yet, he most certainly knew about the plans being laid by the much-lauded Captain Cadell and his *Lady Augusta*.

Randell wanted to get to the Darling junction first. Prize or no prize, he wanted to beat the intrepid sea captain with all his backers and their money, in his game little home-made steamship.

CHAPTER ONE

The Sawpit

IN 1852 GUMERACHA occupied a wedge-shaped block between the upper Torrens and its tributary Kenton Creek. It was scarcely a town, barely even a village, just a scratch on the grasslands of the Adelaide Hills, that tinder-dry vastness with its deep gullies and rounded hills, that draw the eye on into the distance: where banksias grow in twisted stands, and golden wattle trees signal the coming of spring with the purest of yellow blooms.

This tiny settlement had a store, several farms, and the Randell family's stone flour mill. This edifice stood three storeys high, with wings at each end, one for the storage of wheat, the other a mill office. The millstone inside was powered by a stationary steam engine, and sweating stokers fed the firebox and dark smoke poured from the stack. Wagonloads of wheat arrived, poured by the hands of labourers into the mill hoppers. Other teams hauled sacks of flour, away down the Adelaide Road.

Nearby, on the creek bank, stood a shed of bush poles,

clad with branches to keep out the sun. Inside was a saw-pit – six feet deep and three feet wide – lined with walls of loose river stone. Above the pit a heavy river red gum log had been chocked into place. More logs were piled nearby; barked and trimmed, still with the marks of chains where the bullock team had snigged them up. Piles of scantlings lay on the ground, being slowly claimed by the dust.

Two men, stripped of their shirts, worked the pit saw, with its handles perpendicular to the blade. One stood in the pit and one on the log, their biceps and shoulders swelling with the effort of driving the implement. The saw cut only on the down stroke, which allowed the man below to use his weight to assist, but the pit was a hell of heat and falling sawdust, reeking of fresh-cut timber, while hands blistered and tempers frayed. The rounds were first taken off the log, leaving a square flitch, from which boards could be taken off at the desired thickness.

'Halt there,' cried William Randell. 'You're off the line boys.' William was the oldest brother, prime instigator of this venture, and a stickler for accuracy.

'Scarcely a few hundredths,' complained Tom, but still he backed up the blade an inch or two and tried again.

When it started to grow dark, the men packed up, and William was surprised but pleased when a slim figure walked down the track, taking a seat on the stacked eight-inch beams, swinging her sixteen-year-old legs, saying nothing, but humming a popular tune as she watched.

Elliot, Tom, and the two carpenters walked home while

William finished the last of the tidying up. When this was done he sidled across to the girl, wiping his hands on a rag.

'Hello there Bessie, are you back from school?'

Bessie, more properly known as Elizabeth Ann Nickels, beamed, 'Yes, Ebenezer brought me home today. Two whole weeks of freedom – can't complain about that, can I?' She came to her feet easily and looked around. 'You've made progress, in these last months,' she said, and her gaze locked on William. He was twelve years her senior, and she worshipped him. Good looks and an irrepressible character ran in the Randells like gold threads through cloth.

'That we have. In two weeks we'll start carting all the pieces down to the Murray, and put her together.'

'Like a jigsaw puzzle,' Bessie said.

'Yes, exactly that,' he agreed. 'Then she might start looking like a boat at last.'

William was not especially tall, and he was long in the torso and short in the legs. He had never once in his life been able to touch his toes, but was a strong and nimble man nevertheless. He fumbled in his pockets for a tortoiseshell snuff box, and took a pinch with long, artist's fingers.

'Shall I walk you home?' asked Bessie.

'I might look in on the mill as we pass, but we can walk together as far as that, if you want to.'

As they walked Bessie skipped ahead sideways so she could see his face. 'Miss Rowland told me to ask after you,' she said impishly.

'Oh did she?' William grimaced. He and Mary Rowland, the younger of two school mistresses at the Rundle Street Girls' School in Adelaide, had gone perilously close to getting engaged a couple of years earlier. In truth he had viewed the situation with alarm, aware that his natural friendly demeanour had been mistaken for romantic interest.

Bessie's eyes danced. 'I rather think that she's still sweet on you.'

William fumbled for a way of changing the subject. 'And did you do well in your examinations?'

'Well enough to keep Father happy at least,' she smiled. 'Oh it's so tedious, William – apart from English and History – I rather like those. I want to finish with school and start living.'

'I was the same,' he admitted. 'But you'll be done with it soon enough.'

Nearing the mill, William slowed his pace and stopped. 'I'd better check on things in the mill. Perhaps it's best if you get on home.'

'Of course. Will you be at church tomorrow?'

'You can bet on it,' he smiled. And when he reached the side door of the mill he paused and turned back to watch Bessie run down the road towards home. Sunset turned the yellow grass to rich gold, and her hair was the same colour. Bessie was great company, and she brought sunshine and happiness wherever she went.

William's attention was quickly taken as he approached the blacksmith's shop outside the mill, with its glow of fire from the forge, a boiler taking shape from iron sheet, and the muscular form of the blacksmith hammering away. This boiler would one day produce steam for William's river boat, and he walked across to consult with the blacksmith.

The rest of the engine was being manufactured by German-born engineer Mr Claus Gehlkin. It would be an old-style beam engine with a ten-inch cylinder, and a projected output of around seven horsepower. The intention was that the engine would be economical – William did not intend to spend all his time cutting wood on the riverbank to feed the firebox.

William leaned with one hand on the stone wall and closed his eyes for a moment, daydreaming of what his paddle-steamer would be like when she came together. He pictured himself at the tiller, navigating the bends and bars of the great Murray River.

It was strange, but whenever he had that vision, Bessie was always beside him.

CHAPTER TWO

Down to Noa No

W.B. RANDELL, the family patriarch, and the founder of Gumeracha, was not convinced that the paddle steamer 'scheme' would ever turn a profit.

'This boat idea is attractive to ye beys, I can see that,' he told the chief conspirators, William, Tom and Elliot, in his slow but thick Devonshire accent. 'But mind it's no more than a hobby while us attends to the business of our family. That's the proper thing and please don't ee forget it.'

Still, he allowed the brothers leeway to complete their duties while also following their new passion. The next stage of the operation – hauling all the prefabricated boat parts down to the Murray River – had to be undertaken as a normal part of the routine – usually while also droving small mobs of cattle to fatten on the kangaroo grasses and fodder-trees along the banks.

From Gumeracha to the family's property at Noa No was some thirty miles. First a rough trail that followed the River Torrens as far as Narcoonah, then a sharp turn on a south-easterly heading down a road that already bore the family name. This track meandered over and between stony brown hills to the rim of the valley, with views for forty miles across the plains, before reaching the river at Mannum. From there the route detoured northwards along the Murray, past bird-filled lagoons and orange cliffs, to Noa No.

After more than a dozen such trips, the dray loaded down with heavy timber sections and planking, chasing strayed bullocks and horses breaking hobbles and heading for home, enduring broken wheels, bogs and all the other inconveniences of the road, the makings of a paddle steamer lay beside the river in carefully laid out piles.

This makeshift boat yard stood on an isthmus of reed - infested ground between two flood-plain lagoons. They had cleared a wide landing of vegetation, allowing full river access and views up and down the majestic waterway: at mist rising off the surface in the early morning, sunlight dazzling the eyes at noon, and every ripple hiding a moonbeam after dusk.

Each section of the boat was numbered and labelled, but the wood was still green and had, in many cases, swelled or warped. Forcing pieces to fit often required the use of steam, along with persuasive jigs and iron jacks. No stage of the building went smoothly, but slowly the keel and a series of ribs took shape – the gentle and practical lines of a shallow-drafted riverboat.

When the brothers tired of home-butchered beef or

mutton they ate fat murray cod or callop from the set fishing lines Elliott checked morning and night.

One day William and his brothers were fitting planks into the frame when an unusual-looking skiff with a spritsail rig appeared from upstream. At first it appeared as if it would sail on past.

'What the hell is that?' breathed Tom. He was the second-eldest son, and had traditionally been William's partner in all the schemes and adventures the pair could dream up. They knew most of the boats in the area, and this one was out of the ordinary.

'No idea at all,' said William, pausing from his labours to watch the boat, and take a pinch of snuff.

The strange craft looked at first as if it would carry on downstream. Suddenly, however, it tacked and doubled back into the current. Just offshore from the Randell brothers' little boat yard, the crew lowered the sail and sculled into the bank.

The strange vessel, William estimated to be eighteen-feet in length, constructed of what appeared to be tallow-infused canvas stretched over a timber frame. It was crewed by as filthy a mob of desperados as the eldest brother had seen. Three of the four, he guessed correctly, looked more like out-of-luck miners than seamen.

Flanked by Elliot and Tom, William walked to meet the skiff as the crew made her fast to the bank. The man who stepped from the boat and approached the skeleton of the new paddle steamer was tall and broad-shouldered, with a jaw like a wooden strut and a moustache more advanced than the unshaven stubble on the rest of his face.

'Who, may I ask, are you?' the new arrival inquired, removing his cap to reveal a tousled head of hair.

William was aware that he was on home ground; that this man was the interloper. 'Well sir, I might just as easily ask the same question. Who are you?'

'I'm Captain Francis Cadell of Leith, Scotland, sea captain and explorer.'

So this is the famous Francis Cadell, William thought. He bowed from the shoulder, eyes twinkling. 'And I'm William Randell, of Gumeracha, herd boy and errand-runner.'

Ignoring the joke, Cadell's eyes roved the site with deliberate slowness, as if taking in every detail. 'What, may I ask, are you constructing here?'

William Randell was not stupid. The other man's reputation had preceded him. If there was anyone in South Australia likely to get a paddle steamer on the river and collect the government reward money ahead of him, it was Captain Cadell. 'Oh, this? Just a barge, sir.'

Captain Cadell raised one hairy eyebrow. 'A barge? Well what's that?' he said, pointing to a sheet-metal object up on blocks on the other side of the clearing. 'It looks like a strange little boiler.'

William folded his arms across his chest. 'Maybe it is, and maybe it isn't.' To distract Cadell, he approached the skiff, with its crew now stretching their legs on the bank. 'Speaking of strange – I don't think I've yet seen a vessel like this one. I'll hazard a guess and say that it's some kind of transportable boat?'

'You'd be right,' said Cadell.

William went on, 'And you've come from far upstream?'

'Thirteen-hundred miles, all the way downriver from Tyntynder Station, in Victoria,' said Cadell, puffing out his chest. 'We carried the frame on a wagon from Melbourne and up through Bendigo. She's proved to be a stout little vessel, but I'll be happy to be voyaging on the Murray in a more solid craft soon enough.'

'Oh,' said William, 'so you're building something more substantial then?'

'I am. My *Lady Augusta* is on the slips at Chowne's shipyard in Sydney as we speak. Waterline length of a hundred feet – twin engines – forty horsepower all up. A fitting vessel to be the first to navigate the river with steam and collect two thousand pounds from the Government of South Australia.'

William forced a smile. 'Well best of luck then; I've enjoyed our chat but now I'll get back to work, if you don't mind.'

Cadell inclined his head. 'No doubt we shall meet again.'

'No doubt,' said William, watching the crew pile in, with Cadell giving the transom a final shove before clambering aboard and touching his forehead with three extended fingers in a mock salute.

When the strange craft had been rowed out into the

stream, and the sail unfurled, filling with the dry South Australian breeze, William turned to his brothers; 'From now on we'll work night and day. We can't let that Scottish prig beat us.'

CHAPTER THREE

Boiler Trouble

For William and his brothers, hard days and hard weeks followed. They installed lateral stringers to support the hull, then fixed the remaining boards to the frame with iron 'dumps' dipped in tar; laying the timbers edge-to-edge in a manner known as carvel planking. The seams needed to be caulked with oakum to help make them watertight, though William had been warned that leaking was as natural to wooden boats as floating.

Much of the deck was left open to the bilge – better for loading cargo down low, but boards had to be laid and caulked in key areas, including an elevated foredeck and a bench for the tiller man. The boiler and engine had to be installed and secured.

Elliott and Tom went back to Gumeracha for more light timbers several times, for the 'finishing off' was using far more material and taking more time than they had anticipated. William hired casual labourers when he could, and family farm hands were also expected to pick up the tools when not working with livestock.

The three brothers made a strong team. William was the unquestioned boss, with good instincts and a natural sense of fair play. Tom was great with his hands and always reliable, able to stick at a task until was done and done well. Elliott was quick with a joke, the perpetual helper, responding to shouted commands of 'A minute over here please Elliott,' or 'Has anyone got a free hand?' The younger brother's occasional absences to check his fishing lines or to chase a goanna were as forgivable as his appetite for treacle pudding. Above all, the three brothers had a work ethic that drove them from dawn to nightfall, and progress was steady if not remarkable.

Right through the process, however, the three brothers were still expected to play their part in the family business. Tom managed, on behalf of his father, a block of fruit trees, and Elliott was constantly coming and going with cattle. William, too, had responsibilities with the flour mill and sale of timbers from the saw pit. They were also expected to rest on the Sabbath, in line with their strict Baptist upbringing, and to attend services when possible.

By late December, 1852, with the infamous South Australian summer beginning to bite, William fell ill from overwork and obsessive sleeplessness. He returned to Gumeracha to recuperate, worn out and somewhat disillusioned with the size of his undertaking.

Still, the work continued. The absence of one brother was most often compensated for with the arrival of another – the recently married John, or young Ebenezer. William recovered and went back more determined than ever, and the riverside structure was now starting to look like a real boat. By then it was the talk of the river for miles around.

Finally, with half the population of Mannum watching, helping, or hollering useless advice, Tom drove a bullock team, hitched by heavy chain to the hull, into the reedy shallows at Noa No until the water frothed at their chests. The bullocks bellowed with the effort, while the paddle steamer slid on sapling rollers into the water.

'Gee Rogue; up Sergeant; stead-ee, stead-ee,' cried Tom, and the crack of his whip sounded above the shouts and slip of the hull. Meanwhile, his heeler dashed through the shallows nipping at fetlocks and yapping excitedly.

At last, with the boat near to floating free, the team was led ashore, glossy from the water. Now, the brothers began to load their creation up, starting with a ton of three-foot-long dry river red gum logs for the hold, all carried by hand through the shallows and passed up on board. Twice they had to call on the bystanders to help push the craft into deeper water as her draft increased. At this point they deployed anchors bow and stern to hold her length-wise to the current.

Finally, they carried on their personal effects; bedding and tools, while Elliot lit and fed the firebox. The stack streamed grey smoke into a cloudless sky.

William was back on shore, surrounded by several

young female admirers when Elliot gave a loud shriek, then caused a mighty splash as he jumped overboard and headed for dry land at a run.

'What on earth is wrong?' William shouted.

'It's the boiler,' Elliott shouted. 'It's swellin'.'

'Swelling?'

'Yes.'

'Badly?' William asked. The group of young ladies were already beginning to back away.

'Damn ye William. What CAN'T be bad about it?'

'Is it going to blow?'

'I reckon so. Get everyone away from the thing.'

William, however, needed to see the situation with his own eyes. He walked towards the boat, the water almost to his thighs. 'By God you're right,' he called back to Elliott, who was now standing with Tom on the shore. William cursed under his breath, not only had the boiler swollen, but steam and boiling water was leaking through the seams.

'Get away from there,' cried Tom, and William reluctantly began sloshing towards the bank, his dungarees wrapping wetly around his legs.

He was only halfway there when there was a terrible popping sound then a hiss of steam: a cloud that rose to the skies like a thunderhead.

William did not hesitate. He galloped for the bank like a racehorse, accompanied by a howl of laughter from the spectators, who were all now at a safe distance. He didn't stop until he was out of the water, at which point he turned to watch as a jet of steam shot from the boiler to the oohs and aahs of the assembled spectators.

The three brothers hurried on into the safety of the trees, where they finally turned to see a plume of steam on its way to galaxies unknown.

'Well at least she bloody floats,' said Elliott.

William shot his younger brother a look that would have wilted a lesser man. 'Glad you think it's funny,' he said. 'I don't.' And he crossed his arms and stared at their beautiful boat, enveloped in a shroud of smoke like a warship.

CHAPTER FOUR

Captain Cadell

ACCOMPANIED by the crisp sound of my shoes on the teak boards I pace the short distance from the curved bulkhead to my desk. In my hand I hold a letter. Already I have read it three or four times, smarting at the insult contained therein. I, Captain Francis Cadell of Leith, do not take insult lightly, and my lips twist and writhe with the force of words that try to hurl themselves across five hundred miles to the author of that letter.

The captain's cabin of the SS *Cleopatra* feels like a prison to me. Right now I need to be in free, yet I'm chained to my command. I pause in my pacing to look through the observation window across the Town Jetty of Hobson's Bay, Melbourne, where gangs of stevedores are unloading the ship's holds via a derrick, powered by a donkey winding engine. Beyond this, to the east, I see the ruffled waters of Port Phillip Bay and Saint Kilda Beach, a few strollers holding their hats in the wind.

The activities of strangers, and indeed the unloading of

the *Cleopatra* interests me but little. I am the captain of this steamer only for a few months; a stop-gap measure to ensure that my bank account balance is recorded in black ink. Not enough, however, never enough. Money, damned money. A curse or a blessing depending on the lack or surfeit.

I pause to mop my brow with a handkerchief, then sit at my desk to read the letter one last time, hearing the voice, as I read, of Thomas Chowne, boatbuilder of Pyrmont, Sydney.

Resolved to action at last, I pick up and trim a quill, dip the nib in my ink pot and address an envelope to that most useful but wooden human being, Mr William Younghusband of Adelaide, South Australia.

After a pensive moment, listening to the shouts of the stevedore gangs deep in the steamer and on the pier, I begin to write.

> My Dear William
>
> Forgive me for getting quickly to the import
> of this letter, but you and I have known
> each other and worked for each other's
> interests for some five years now. I must tell
> you that those very interests are
> threatened, and threatened harshly.
>
> As of this moment, I am in Melbourne with
> the *Cleopatra*. As soon as our cargo is
> discharged, probably Thursday, we will

embark passengers and load goods bound for Sydney. There, as you know, at Chowne's Shipyards at Pyrmont, lies our almost finished vessel, the *Lady Augusta*, which we both know will one day be the pride of the Murray River. The launch party is scheduled for a date just a few weeks from now – for which event I have lined up a bevy of dignitaries, along with an attractive and well-connected young lady to swing the bottle (Miss Williams will wear an eye-catching dress of my favourite colour – blue, she assures me), followed by a repast fit for the gods.

At the thought of the delightful Miss Williams in a blue dress I allow myself a pause. I have aspirations concerning this young woman, but that base desire is nowhere near as important as the cause of this letter. I force my mind back to the issue at hand and continue to write.

What is the problem? I hear you ask. My answer is twofold.

The first issue is that I am in receipt of a letter from my boatbuilder Thomas Chowne, demanding an overdue progress payment of two thousand pounds. If this amount does not reach his bank account in ten days' time, he will cancel the contract and place our beautiful new paddle steamer in the hands of auctioneers. Demand for river vessels is apparently strong on the Hunter, Manning, Macleay and other rivers north of Sydney.

The second problem is that I do not have two thousand pounds, or even a fair portion of it, being fully stretched in all directions.

Now, as you know, the Legislative Council of South Australia has offered a prize of exactly that amount to the first two mariners to navigate the Murray as far as Swan Hill. In doing so they set conditions that made it possible for only a very specific kind of vessel to succeed in claiming the prize. Strangely, they have specified an iron hull, and the reason for this escapes me completely.

As you also know, in anticipation of liquidity problems, I wrote to the Governor, Mr Young, and asked him, that in addition to the prize already offered, we might enter into a second, more private agreement. The terms of which are as follows: £500 to bring the Lady Augusta through the bar,

£1000 to steam up to the Darling Junction, and £250 per quarter to operate as a trading entity on the river for the first twelve months.

For reasons known only to himself, Governor Young has not yet accepted this generous offer. He has obfuscated, delayed and bedevilled me at every turn. This is where I require your assistance. I implore you to use every force of persuasion at your disposal to get Young to accept this arrangement. Your position on the Legislative Council will make it impossible for him to ignore you, particularly if you can enlist allies into our cause. Promise him a berth on our inaugural voyage up the Murray if you have to. Promise him anything that I have in my power to deliver.

The moment that I receive your return letter with the news that Governor Young has signed the agreement, a discreet firm of financiers here in Melbourne will provide me with a loan for the amount of two thousand pounds. I will place a teller's cheque in the hands of Thomas Chowne when I reach Sydney, and the launch will go ahead, bringing excellent publicity and the beginnings of this great new venture.

I do not need to remind you of the glory and wealth that awaits us as inaugurators of the river trade. A million pounds worth of wool a year can be moved on that river. Haulage fees for such a vast fortune will make us rich.

I also don't need to remind you of the ragtag band of hill-brothers who are cobbling together their own vessel near Mannum. The blow to our pockets and reputations if they are allowed to beat us to the trade will be both insulting and irretrievable. I await your urgent response. Abraham Knott, master of the *Norwood* will wait off Port Adelaide for your written reply, up to forty-eight hours he promises me, then fly with the nor'easterlies back to me with the answer. Please do not let this crucial task take longer.

Yours

Francis Cadell (Captain)

After putting the quill back in the holder, I lift the two pages up to waft in the candle heat to dry them. This done, I fold them into the envelope, then raise the brass bell from the desk and toll it lustily.

The lad who hurries in a few moments later stands at attention. He is a slow-witted specimen, though reliable. 'Yes, Captain, sir?'

'Take two men and a skiff. I need this letter rowed across to the master of the fast schooner *Norwood*, do you know it?'

'Yes sir.'

'And hurry. They sail for Adelaide with the tide.'

The lad takes the package and leaves. Now I breathe at last, leaning on my desk with one hand, allowing myself to think forward to the launch of the *Lady Augusta*, and the blue dress of Miss Williams.

CHAPTER FIVE

The First Run

WILLIAM RANDELL inspected the near-ruined boiler with a sinking heart. The firebox had been formed with copper sheet, and the searing-hot river red gum fire had scorched and melted its way through, leading to the catastrophic mixing of water and heat inside the boiler. Amazingly, the main body of the unit was still intact.

'We're lucky we didn't blow everyone up,' said William, taking a frustrated pinch of snuff and turning to sneeze. Recovering his equanimity, he turned to Elliot. 'Would you ride for home and bring back everything we'll need – iron plate, bolts and tools. I'll make a list. If Father will allow you the wagonette that would be quickest – you could be back by tomorrow afternoon at a pinch.'

While he and Tom waited for his younger brother's return, William could scarcely keep away from the boiler, even after it had been stripped of all the ruined material and cleaned to bright metal with a wire brush. 'Building the firebox from copper was a blunder,' he said to Tom, 'but

I'd have thought that quarter inch steel plate would be sufficient for the boiler itself.'

'It were expanding,' said Tom. 'You saw for yourself.'

William said little in reply but at least they had the final fit-out of the paddle-steamer's cabins to keep them busy. In between tasks they swam in the river and attended to Elliot's set-lines.

The younger brother returned the following afternoon in a farm wagonette, the springs near inverted with weight, the horses blown and hunting for water. Grinning from cheek to freckled cheek, Elliott climbed to the rear of the vehicle and threw off a canvas tarpaulin. 'I brought enough steel plate to rebuild the firebox – hand auger, drill bits, files an' bits 'n' bobs.'

William grinned, and reached up to grip his brother's hand. 'Well done boy, you've got a full machine shop back in there. Let's get to work then.'

Elliott paused, 'That's not all I'm bringing. Father's 'ad news of Captain Cadell. Ee's done a deal with the governor to be first with a boat on the river, for a two-thousand pound reward, staged payments for getting' through the bar, up to the Darling then running a freight service for twelve months.'

William whistled, 'Where's our two thousand pounds?'

'It's all about connections, boys,' said Tom. 'Cadell has the right friends.'

'Not only that,' Elliot went on, 'But his new paddle steamer is named after the Governor's wife – the *Lady*

Augusta, and she's to be launched in Pyrmont, Sydney in just a few weeks.'

'The mongrel! Is it ready so soon?' cried William. 'Let's not waste a minute. We'll be first on the river, but we need to be first to the Darling too.'

Less than a week later, without an audience this time, and under a benign sun and a breeze that smelled of autumn, Elliot lit a blaze in the firebox of the rebuilt boiler, beginning with small sticks and scrap timber. They'd done their best with the refurbishment, drilling holes with a brace and bit, and installing bolts instead of rivets.

Yet, Elliot was still wary. As the boiler's glass showed sufficient water, and the pressure gauge slowly flicked upwards towards a working pressure of thirty pounds-per-square-inch, he jumped overboard and headed for the bank. From a safe distance the three brothers watched as the boiler reached full pressure.

'It's holding together,' said William hopefully, but even from the bank he could see that it was again swelling appreciably.

'Maybe we should have used half inch plate,' said Elliot.

William shook his head. 'If so we'd have had a lot more trouble fixing her – drilling holes in quarter inch steel was bad enough.' After a long pause he fixed a cautiously pleased expression on his face, 'Swelling or no swelling – she's holding. Let's take her for a test run. Then ... I've got an idea.'

With the boiler still swelling and beginning to leak at the seams the three brothers threw off her lines and leapt aboard. It was Elliot's job now to prepare the engine for its first run, 'oiling 'round' and checking the gauges.

Then, while Tom tidied the lines and stowed the ground-tackle William opened the regulator and grinned as the engine cycled for the first time.

It was a beam-engine, operating through a process beginning with steam jetting into the single cylinder, which was jacketed with timber for insulation. The piston moved upwards in response, forcing the overhead beam upwards on that side and down on the other. The movement of a slide valve, operated by an eccentric wheel-driven shaft, allowed steam into the opposite end of the cylinder, thus forcing the piston to move in the other direction. Down came the beam. This cycle delivered reciprocal motion to a connecting rod at the other end of the beam, which applied rotary force to the crankshaft.

It was an old design, even in 1853, but Mr Claus Gehlkin knew his stuff, and the engine was made to last. With a breathless rush, both port and starboard paddlewheels started to churn in their shells, bringing up the smell of river water so it was thick in their nostrils.

The paddle wheels worked perfectly – three paddles immersed at any time – one almost vertical and two others either entering or leaving the water. Somehow, through luck and diligence they had got it right – including transferring enough torque from the engine to move the vessel along.

William punched one fist into the air and shouted an old school scrimmaging cry, using the rudder to steer the brand-new vessel into the current, facing it mightily. Within a few minutes the little paddle steamer was making two-and-a-half knots upriver, while grey teals and black ducks left staccato patterns on the river surface as they winged away from their path.

'It works,' cried William to his brothers, and there was a pricking of tears in his eyes. 'The first steamer on the River Murray!' This fact was true for all to see, with smoke streaming from the stack, and steam escaping in puffs with each stroke of the piston.

'Indeed she is,' said Tom. 'But now look, she needs a name. You've been cagey about what to call her?'

Elliot took up the cry from his place near the engine astern. 'A working steam boat needs a name. What will we call her?'

'I would've thought that obvious,' said William. 'There's only one fitting name that I can think of.'

Tom grinned, 'I'm guessing you want to name her after Ma? The *Mary Ann*?'

'That's it,' said William. 'Just what I was thinking.'

'The *Mary Ann* it is,' agreed Elliot, 'and you're right, there's no better name in all the world.

It was a special day for William, as he continued to steer this wonderful creation of theirs, for he was learning that the steamer now had a life and personality of its own – and experiencing the river by boat was always interesting. He saw a shepherd on the bank with his flock taking water on a shallow spit, a couple of travellers camped on the eastern shore and a Narraltie man spear-fishing in the shallows. The beauty of the river stretched dreamily into the distance, gilded with the realisation that the adventure was only just beginning.

Over the next three hours the engine gained and lost power as Elliot walked a tightrope between threatening to blow the boiler apart with too much heat, or to underfeed it through cautiousness. Tom divided his time between running repairs and sounding the channel with a lead line. William was already marking depths on a sketch-chart, as well as listing issues that would need attention when they returned to their makeshift boathouse.

It was an important first journey, and on their return to Noa No, William put his plan for improving the boiler into action. The three brothers dragged heavy bullock-chains aboard, then wrapped them tightly around the boiler, using shackles to secure them. As a finishing touch, they used a sledgehammer to pound heavy timber wedges in between chain and boilerplate to make it tighter still.

When it was done, the three brothers lounged on the deck, while William produced a single bottle of ale, brewed in Oakbank in the Adelaide Hills, the brewer's name, Johnston, stamped on the brown glass bottle.

This was a rare treat for the boys, for whom alcohol was

rarely, if ever, consumed, their father and Baptist church both being opposed to its consumption. WB Randell, in fact, proudly referred to himself, in his Devonshire way, as a 'taytottler.'

'Beer? Father would kill us,' said Elliot.

'Ar there, steady on. What he don't know won't hurt him, and it's just a small mug each — something special after what we've been through.'

Jar in hand Elliot stood back and regarded the newly-wrapped boiler. 'Looks jerry-built, but I can't deny that it will be stronger.'

Tom turned to William, 'What's next?'

William scowled, 'If Cadell can extort money out of the South Australian government, so can we. I'll write a letter to Governor Young meself and see what we can get.'

CHAPTER SIX

Scouting the Bar

THE SLIP AND GLIDE of the oars, and the flap of the sails soothes my heart as we sail and row down the Goolwa Channel, with Hindmarsh Island to port, and the isthmus of low sand, shearwater nests and spinifex that separates us from a raging sea to starboard. Six stout men on board and the whaleboat is filled to the gunnels with equipment. The sounds of quiet talk, and the cries of birds combine to sooth my soul, for I am in turmoil inside. I am angry, helplessly angry, for things in recent days have not gone my way.

That foolish boatbuilder, Henry Chowne, upon my arrival in Sydney, and after accepting my cheque for two thousand pounds – so hard won from my deal with the South Australian Government and through the agency of a Melbourne moneylender – showed me a glaringly incomplete *Lady Augusta* and admitted that we would have to delay the launch. God how I hate delays.

My dear Captain Cadell, he had said. *I thank you for the receipt of the two-thousand-pound progress payment. Unfortunately, I have bad news. Men of all trades are deserting my employ and heading for the Australian goldfields and this is causing chaos in the yard. I'm sure you understand that this makes it difficult ...*

What fool of a man cannot keep his tradesmen from chasing dreams of millionairedom in far flung wildernesses? I hear also that Chowne is mixed up in business problems; lawsuits and such with his brothers. That kind of thing I have no patience for.

He attempted to talk me around to a launch date in April, but after a torrid argument we settled on March 24. Even then my new flagship will not be fully finished – the engines not installed at that stage and some of the fitout incomplete.

Forced to resume my duties as master of the *Cleopatra*, I steamed back to Adelaide via Melbourne with the usual cargoes and tedious passengers at the captain's table. My problems worsened at Port Adelaide when the fool of a pilot, John Taylor by name, refused to let me take the *Cleopatra* ashore to have her hull scrubbed – a sorely needed procedure. Once he had been rowed off towards the shore I admit that my temper got the better of me.

I took it upon myself to take the steamer in, ordered forward revolutions and set off. It was then that the cockswain of a nearby boat called out that our screw had contacted a disused mooring chain (where I do not believe any mooring should have been) and had fouled.

I called on the mate to investigate, and after a glance

over the stern he replied that he was not convinced that the screw was foul, and that we should try again. Thanks to this irresponsible report I ordered forward revolutions again, at which point the screw, but lightly wrapped at that stage became fully entangled. Oh, what embarrassment for a man such as I, with passengers, crew, and neighbouring boats all laughing at this misfortune.

I did, of course, protest directly to Governor Young of the incompetence of the port authorities in leaving a disused mooring hidden under the water. The said authorities, however, counter attacked by launching an inquiry. This kangaroo-court decided that by moving my ship, after she had been moored and secured by a licensed pilot, I had violated No. 2 Schedule A of the Ordinance No. 3 or some such rot, and thereby incurred a penalty of £20. You can imagine how the fires of my rage are burning at this.

Even now, heading down the Goolwa Channel, my face reddens with the memory. But like any man of action, I am determined that the delay while a team of divers from Fiji work to untangle the mess will be worthwhile, for with the *Cleopatra* going nowhere for several days I planned and executed a hurried trip down to the Goolwa.

Of all the things on my mind over the first four months of 1853, first and foremost is a dangerous beast, capricious and capable of murder on a whimsy. I know a killer when I meet one, and the bar of the River Murray has killed ships and men before. We go forth to help ensure the *Lady Augusta*'s safe passage.

This will be my second attempt to scout out the treacherous and narrow channels hidden amongst the breaking surf and pressure waves. The first was undertaken in January, in a government skiff we carried overland from Encounter Bay, in the company of my agent William Younghusband, the pilot from Port Eliot and three stout oarsmen.

We ran out through the bar, taking white water over the bow, and showing our bravado, plying the ash blades like Hercules powered our left arms and Achilles the right. Safely we rode the swells back through to the calm, holding position, broaching down the face of several waves but this was easily corrected with the oars.

Fired with salt-lust and courage I decided to repeat the adventure, steering us again for the break. This time, meeting a much larger set of waves than before, we came unstuck.

Every true mariner has felt the gut swooping fear when he sees the green glassy slopes of the wave that he knows will bring mayhem and destruction on the boat in his charge. This knowledge comes long before the event, for in a seaman's mind always is the capabilities of his vessel. After this realisation there is nothing but prayer and hope; that some quirk of the sea or the hand of God will intervene.

Not this time. Our skiff was grasped in the jaws of that

wave as if in the fangs of some seaborne tiger. The boat rolled and all six aboard were dumped into the wild cold seas. Fully clothed as we were, this was a disaster. The next wave, it seemed was even larger, picking me up bodily and twisting me around.

Thankfully we all made it onto the beach alive, and to assuage my shame I told myself that in a well-found whaleboat (like the one I am in now), with a crew of scurvy fellows the capsize would not have happened, but it was true that I'd taken a knock to my pride, and for many nights I experienced terrible dreams of the *Lady Augusta*, my new riverboat, rolling on that same wave, my hopes and dreams of a fleet to trade up and down the length of the Murray River torn asunder. And as the months passed I realised that the scant knowledge of the bar that I had gained in that disastrous foray were useless, for the channels change almost weekly.

Now, with the *Cleopatra* in Adelaide until the morrow, I have recruited men to camp on the beach here, study and mark the channels so that we will know the way in when I return with the *Lady Augusta*. At least then something good might come of these weeks of bad fortune.

Ahead we see the high ground of Barker's Knoll and Observation Hill, and it is on the beach below this small peak, that tents will be pitched for my observers who will watch and buoy the mouth – that half-mile gape of the great river.

In several weeks' time I must cross this terrible stretch

of water with a river boat not made for such a place — a river boat has no vee in the hull — no grip on the water. But the paradox is that I must bring the *Lady Augusta* through or give up all hope of glory.

I hear that Randell is coming to Goolwa with his home-made steamer in less than one week, and dearly I would love to stay and view that odd little creation in its final form. Yet the *Cleopatra* must sail with tomorrow's tide for Port Melbourne and Sydney, just in time for our delayed launch date.

Now, as the stem of the whaleboat thumps into the beach, and we unload stores, pitch tents, and say our farewells to those who will stay behind, I can smell the inland borne on that river. For me it is the smell of future wealth. Dare I hope, an empire?

CHAPTER SEVEN

The Governor's Gift

WILLIAM RANDELL had a pleasant surprise when a letter came back from the governor's office, on official letterhead, with the following response:

> We applaud your initiative, and your desire to begin trade on the River Murray. We ask you to take your vessel to Goolwa, on Thursday next, where we would like to review the vessel and reward you appropriately for your endeavours. We also require that any cargo be inspected for customs purposes.

'In other words,' drawled Tom, 'they'll award us some paltry amount then claim it back in customs levies.'

'Still,' mused William, 'at least the governor is taking us seriously.'

While they prepared for the journey downriver, Ebenezer arrived from Gumeracha with a load of flour for cargo, and a box of fruit for the dignitaries who would board the *Mary Ann* in Goolwa. These were all grown on the family property – apples, pears, peaches, and golden-drop plums.

With a hired man joining them as general deckhand and stoker they set off on the eighty river miles to Goolwa, including the crossing of a violent Lake Alexandrina. Steering into the teeth of a twenty-five-knot southerly wind was a sobering experience for William, the waters of the shallow lake whipped into short-period swells that broke over the bow, and filled their eyes and lips with salt.

William checked constantly that the canvas covers over the flour bags were wrapped tight, for water was the enemy of bagged flour, and the valuable cargo could not be wasted.

The *Mary Ann*, forced to prove her mettle in conditions she had not been designed for, showed that despite her shallow draft, she could maintain steerage in anything the Murray threw at her. Even so, the vessel's speed bled away to the point that it became impossible for her to reach Goolwa on the appointed day.

'The Governor will wait for us until tomorrow at least,' William promised as the crew powered on through a blustery night. They took bleary-eyed turns at the tiller and the bilge-pump, or resting in 'nests' amongst the flour, finally rounding Point Stuart and anchoring in the relative calm of Goolwa Channel after dawn, damp but unbowed by the experience. Each of the brothers managed a few hours' sleep before ensuring that the *Mary Ann* looked her best, with bird dung and dust cleaned away with buckets and sponges.

They steamed into Goolwa, to the pounding blasts of an unexpected nineteen-gun-salute from the cannons on the quay. 'Hell and all,' cried William. 'Nineteen guns, and look at that crowd!'

Not only was Governor Young waiting on the wharf with his wife and official entourage, but there was also a large contingent of spectators. They were mostly well-dressed local gentlemen and ladies, with daughters like dutiful shadows and boys in suits running rampant. Finely-groomed hounds on leashes growled at dock-side mongrels.

As the *Mary Ann* steamed gently alongside, wharfmen tied her snugly to the bollards. And while Governor Young greeted the intrepid Randells warmly, a catering team set up trestles and plates of hams, pickled tongue and baked vegetables, while customs officers gravely counted flour bags.

In addition to the meal prepared by professional cooks, the young ladies of Goolwa had been cooking for several days. Dressed in gowns befitting a ballroom, they came armed with a feast of cakes, confectionaries, and pastries, throwing admiring glances at the intrepid Randell brothers.

Governor Young mounted a dais, with the band conductor's baton pausing mid stroke. His Excellency spoke of progress, made a lot of Captain Cadell's boat that would soon be on its way, and pointed to a barge being constructed for the Scottish Captain at the Winsby Brothers' boatyard adjacent to the wharf, cheekily flying a new flag that would 'become the symbol and pride of Murray River navigators.'

Governor Young then heartily congratulated the 'back-country ingenuity' of the Randell boys and the industriousness of South Australia's children that would one day make the state great. He promised to make available the sum of three hundred pounds, drawn from the Crown moiety of the Land Fund, to be mailed at a later date, as a sign of encouragement and a reward.

The meal went well – the Gumeracha fruit being a particular favourite, and the men who complimented William on both the boat and the food were names he had seen in the newspapers since his youth, but never dreamed of meeting like this. Apart from His Excellency the Lieutenant-Governor and Lady Young, there was Mr Torrens, the Colonial Treasurer, Mr Finniss the Colonial Secretary, Mr John Morphett, Speaker of the Legislative Council and all their wives, along with some dutiful sons and daughters. William found himself the object of attention of both Lady Augusta and a Mrs Maturin, who appeared to be as flirtatious as she was highly placed.

When the repast was finished, the official party, led by His Excellency and Lady Augusta, walked the gangway into the *Mary Ann* and examined the rough but solid carpentry that characterised the vessel.

Elliot had artfully ensured that the boiler pressure was so low so that no sign remained of expanding metal or steam hissing through seams, but the chain-wrapped boiler caught even the Governor's eye. 'That one won't get away from you, Mr Randell,' he commented drily, and it took William some moments to understand that the taciturn Governor had just made a joke.

When the festivities were over, and the tables and remaining food removed, there was a shaking of hands all around, and the band played as the *Mary Ann* steamed at a sedate pace away from the wharf.

At the tiller, William was quiet and thoughtful, inspired by this entrance into the higher echelons of the Colony. The Governor had said that the 'Murray River would one day be a canal of commerce, alive with steamboats of all kinds, bearing passengers and goods into the interior, and the wealth of a nation back to Mother England for the glory of the empire.' At that moment, proud and excited, steering out into a beam sea, William could almost see that future unfold before his eyes.

Later, past the lake and in the calm of the river, Tom joined him, and together they enjoyed the serenity of a river sunset.

'So we can head off for the Darling now?' asked the younger brother.

'That we can. But how about a family day first. I know Father's been itching to get down for a look.'

'Good thinking.' Tom smiled. ''Tis strange. Father was never a dyed-in-the-wool supporter of the boat, yet I've a feeling that he's proud of us now.'

'I think so too,' said William. 'And I'm proud that we have made him proud.'

CHAPTER EIGHT

The Family Picnic

IT WAS MARCH the 18th, 1853, when the Randell family gathered at Noa No on the Murray. The station had always been a family outpost, a satellite in their growing economic constellation. It was a perfect location for fattening cattle and escaping summer's heat with swimming holes and sailing skiffs. It was not, however, as well appointed as the homestead at Kenton Park in Gumeracha.

The guests arrived in a trap, a wagonette and a carriage. WB Randell, the patriarch, was indeed proud of his sons as he spotted the paddle steamer at rest. Mary Ann Randell sat beside him, along with their seventh son Samuel, and their daughter Hannah, wife of local clerk Alfred Swaine.

The guests also included the family rouseabout from Kenton Park, Allan Ross, along with school teachers Miss Jane and Miss Mary Ellen Rowland. These two were old family friends – daughters of land agent and accountant, Charles Rowland. Also in the party was a Mr Henry Jamieson, visiting from his holdings upriver.

Smiling from the bench seat of the carriage, talking happily with Ebenezer, was Bessie Nickels, her eyes already searching out the commanding figure of William on the riverbank. He and his brothers were welcoming the first of the guests, fielding exclamations of delight and admiration of the paddle steamer floating alongside the landing.

WB Randell looked the vessel up and down from the shore. 'You beys 'ave done a proper job here. Ye can be proud of yeselves.'

'It's as well we have, for Cadell will be here all too soon,' said William as he strode to meet his mother. 'So what do you think?' he asked her.

'It's beautiful,' she said.

'Now cover your eyes,' he instructed, and when she had done so the deckhand pulled aside a strip of canvas that had been strung to hide the paddle steamer's name. The elder brother walked his mother up close to the boat in the meantime. 'Now open them.'

Mary Ann Randell opened her eyes and burst out, 'Ye sweet things, ee named yer boat for ye mither.'

Tom, Elliot and Samuel escorted the group across their makeshift boat yard, and to the gang plank that would allow them to board. Meanwhile, the boiler steamed and hissed, and the deckhand shoved in another log and slammed the firebox door shut.

William climbed aboard and stood on the foredeck. From there he had the luxury of watching the guests board. His eyes rested on Bessie. She was growing up more every time he saw her. Very much the young lady, but still lively and spirited. His father, bearded and distinguished and his mother, handsome and sharp as a pin, followed.

The Rowland sisters were either side of thirty, always conservatively but finely attired, both bright and interesting, well-read and speaking apropos of the latest news. Yet William found their presence claustrophobic. He did not believe that he had encouraged Mary Ellen's romantic interest in any way, apart from a polite friendship, and somehow it seemed that an 'understanding' had grown up, that he and she might marry. Rather than saying anything, he had simply let the situation draw out for so long that it became obvious that no proposal would be forthcoming.

Now, showing neither favour nor disfavour, he welcomed the guests aboard, and settled them on the timber bench seats that sat where the flour bags had been (now waiting in a vermin-proof shed for their first foray upriver. Bessie however, had no intention of sitting with the other passengers, instead she took her place beside William at the tiller, flushed and excited at the excursion.

When the guests were settled William made a show of issuing nautical commands to his brothers and they hurried with the lines, while keeping the boiler at a low and very safe pressure.

'Full ahead,' bawled William, and Tom opened the regulator to push steam into the cylinder.

Smiling at Bessie, William swung the tiller in a wide arc

and thereby took the *Mary Ann* into the main stream of the wide brown river.

They steamed the twelve miles down to Wall Station, owned by the Baker family, and the hours passed with the sunshine brilliant on orange ridges and stately red gums, the old river monarchs. Bessie scarcely drew breath, telling William of her plans for when she had finished school.

'Just six months and I'll be all grown up,' she said. 'I've already had some offers of work. Miss Rowland, the younger, that is, thinks that I should become a school teacher, and Mrs Swaine thinks I could make a good seamstress.'

'And which would you prefer?' asked William.

'Neither,' she said. 'I'd rather do what you're doing.'

William grinned, 'You'd like to captain your own steamer?'

'Maybe,' she smiled back.

Later, however, when they landed on the jetty at Wall Station and strolled ashore, William found himself walking next to the elder Rowland sister.

'It's not becoming, you know,' said Miss Jane Rowland.

'What isn't?'

'You and that child, Bessie, flirting.'

'She's sixteen, that's hardly a child, and we're not flirting. We're friends.'

'A man of near thirty, really?'

'I'm only twenty-nine, and I just told you. We're friends.'

'My sister Mary Ellen is still … receptive to any advance you might make.' She stared. 'Time's running out for her, you know. As it already has for me.'

It was food for thought, and William wondered if he was doing Bessie a disservice by encouraging her. Worse, was he doing something patently wrong? After lunch he sought her out alone.

'I hope I haven't given you the wrong idea,' he said. 'We're just friends, right?'

'Of course. I know that,' said Bessie. 'I'm not a silly child.'

Back at Noa No, the party hunted up the horses and turned for home. Elliot went with them as an extra driver. It was a strange thing, but when he returned the following day he said to William.

'Did anything happen with Bessie the other day?'

'No. Why?'

'She damned near cried all the way back to Gumeracha. Wouldn't tell me a thing about what was wrong.'

William looked at the ground and shuffled his feet.

CHAPTER NINE

The Blue Dress

WHAT A DAY it is, here in Pyrmont! The waters of Johnston's Bay glimmer in the sun, with views across to the Glebe Island grain wharf and Balmain. The glittering Miss Williams in her blue dress draws our eyes like a diamond in our midst.

I, Captain Francis Cadell stroll through the crowd of dignitaries who have gathered here, more for the promise of food and drink at my expense than the launch of the strange vessel on the slips.

Thomas Chowne and I share a glance. Now that he has my money, or should I say that of my Melbourne money-lender, we are at peace. I am again the famous Captain Cadell, explorer, sea captain and adventurer.

The band of the 11th Regiment play *Rule Britannia* as my eyes fall on the creation of my designing pen and their steam-saws and adzes. The *Lady Augusta* in the slips, ready to ride the rails.

I swallow a lump of misapprehension. It is true that Thomas Chowne and his men did a sound job of the hull, albeit with delays, and some public infighting between the brothers that I know much more about now than I did when I placed the order. Yet I, the man who had designed one of the most beautiful clipper ships in existence, the *Queen of Sheba*, can scarcely believe that I have had a part in creating such an ill-favoured monster as this. For the *Lady Augusta* is, I have to admit, an ugly boat – and I know that many of the people on the quay that day think the same, though the whispers are too soft for me to hear.

That ugliness is partly because her hundred-foot length of deck is crowded with accommodations. This is a commercial necessity. In extracting the required contract from the Governor, my partner Younghusband promised him a trip on the first voyage. Younghusband himself would have to be there, along with his wife and two daughters. The list goes on. All these people have to be accommodated, and in the style to which they are accustomed. Shallow drafted riverboats have no room below decks, so everything is crammed on top.

I know that it is a dog of a boat – as ugly as any ever launched, but later, these excess cabins can be removed, and her appearance will alter for the better. What will I care? By then I'll carry goods the length and breadth of the river, making money from settlers, miners and farmers desperate for stores.

My mind comes back to the moment, admiring the delectable Miss Williams – that svelte female form in a figure-hugging dress. At least, I decide, I have a handsome young woman to launch my paddle steamer. She fusses and giggles in her shining garb, standing beside a silk-covered bottle suspended by a blue silk sash.

'I name this boat, the *Lady Augusta*,' she cries in a bird-like voice, and the new vessel slides down into the water. This is a nervous moment, for I have seen many a calamity on the slipways of my native Louth, on the Firth of Forth, and it is good to see this bastard lady float at last.

My new paddle steamer rides high in the water, being unladen, and still lacking her boiler and engines, now being finished up in Sussex Street by George Russell and company, who perform their role much more professionally than this fool of a boatbuilder.

It is Chowne himself who takes up the cry. 'Three cheers for the *Lady Augusta* and Captain Cadell.' The crew of the *Esmerelda*, floating alongside, join in.

I feel my heart swell with pride. Yes, it is I who will soon be on the River Murray, and that waterway will become the Mississippi of this country, and riches will rain down upon me.

The *Cleopatra*, the vessel of which I am currently captain, comes alongside to take the *Lady Augusta* in tow so our guests can experience her on the water. And once they are on board the caterers bring on a feast that has cost my backers dear but I assured them was necessary. I sit next to Miss Williams, and her body is a writhing snake inside that dress.

We toast Prince Albert, and the Queen. Chowne, his

tongue hanging out of his mouth like an overgrown dog, raises a toast to Miss Williams.

Much later, back in my cabin on the *Cleopatra*, the blue dress rustles as it hits the floor, and my future seems very bright indeed.

CHAPTER TEN

The Big Bend

'WHAT ON EARTH are you goin' to do with that thing?'

Elliot Randell was sitting on the load of flour that filled the *Mary Ann*'s decks, watching while William ran a whetstone along the blade of a sword – a fearsome weapon some three feet long, with a two-handed hilt, and filigree on the guard.

'You may well ask,' William replied, hefting the weapon. 'I'll use it to defend the *Mary Ann* from all manner of dangers as we delve upriver.' He was quite proud of the sword – given to him by a friend – no doubt a family heirloom that had been hosting spider webs in a corner for years.

The newest of the two deckhands they had hired was just sixteen years, green and raw, straight off the farm, and he happened around the engine, just in time to hear his captain's declaration.

'D-d-dangers?' the lad stammered. 'What kind do you mean?'

William stood up and pointed the weapon towards the north. 'Oh, proper terrible dangers,' he said, with a twinkle in his eye. 'River pirates for a start! And who knows? Armed colonies of Jacobite revolutionaries perhaps.'

'Pirates … revolutionaries? You're joking, aren't you?'

'Not at all, but more than that, there'll be hordes of painted warriors all competing to cut our throats. First the Meru, then the Danggali, the Latje Latje, the Kureinji—' He lowered the point to the deck. 'Oh I'd reckon that this sword will've proved its worth by the time we win our way back south.'

'Win our way?' gulped the young deckhand.

'Yes, an' of course we may lose a man or two.'

The young deckhand disappeared aft, leaving William chuckling to himself.

It was March the twenty-fourth, and the Randell brothers had packed the last of their flour into the hold and prepared for a morning departure. William was feeling cocky, but he put down the sword and looked at Elliot seriously.

'I can't wait to finally get away. We've got the jump on that damned Captain Cadell, by a couple of months at least. He may have launched his *Lady Augusta*, but the engines aren't in her yet, and then he's got to bring her all the way around by sea, then cross the bar. We'll not only get to the Darling Junction before him, but will sell every damn bag of flour in our holds and be back here before he steams into Goolwa.'

'Unless the boiler does blow up on us,' observed Elliot drily. Keeping that leaking iron vessel in one piece remained his primary concern.

'There's that,' admitted William. A moment later there was a terrific splash, and the sound of a man churning through the water towards the riverbank. It was the young deckhand, all his belongings in a hastily gathered bundle, heading for the shore at a rate of knots.

'Well done,' called Tom. 'You just scared our new man off with that damned sword of yours.'

William looked down at the weapon then shrugged. 'Good Christ forgive me. I was only joking.'

By midmorning the next day, Elliot was busy heating the boiler, and they cast off the lines at noon. The river was full of promise over those early miles, and the engine cycled smoothly. They made a good three knots at first, and the deck was a cheerful place, all smiles and jokes, with the sun on the water and the hinterland beckoning.

By the time they had reached the village of Nildottie, however, there were worrying signs – mud bars across half of the river, and shallow treacherous channels that required painstaking attention to navigate.

'It's damn shallow,' said Elliot, but by evening they had passed through the 'Big Bend,' an important milestone, and a place of dramatic scenery, where limestone cliffs, pockmarked with caves, lined the great river's banks.

William declared that reaching the Big Bend was worthy

of issuing a glass of beer all round, a new institution that was always accompanied with a muttered, 'Now then you fellows ... remember not to tell Father.' When the remaining deckhand asked if he might have another measure, they stared at him as if he were a drunkard. Beer, to them, was a special treat, not a staple.

That night they moored on a riverside tree, and hollowed out their own places amongst the flour sacks to sleep. There was no cabin, but underneath the canvas overlay there was plenty of room to sleep, and more space could easily be made my moving a sack or two.

On the second and third days the river became ever shallower. They steamed on, at a crawl, and in desperation pulled into the bank and unloaded several tons of supplies, caching them on the riverbank. This helped, for a time.

Finally, at Penn's Reach, there was no way through. They charged the shallows with the engine thumping, and the paddlewheels throwing spray, but they made no headway. They waded ahead for hundreds of yards through water never deeper than their knees. The *Mary Ann* drew three feet, even after removing much of her burden.

By dusk of that evening William sat in the bow with his legs hanging over the edge, his two brothers beside him. 'I'm afraid we has no choice but to turn back,' he said, 'an' wait for a fresh in the river. It just weren't fated to be this time.'

'We'll have to come back when she rises,' agreed Tom reluctantly.

William thought of Cadell with all his power and official backing, being so close on their heels. He could have cried with frustration. After all their work, and overcoming great difficulties, this seemed like a cruel trick – to have set out not only at the worst time of year, but in a period of drought into the bargain.

Arriving back in Noa-No after three difficult days, with boiler problems as well as the shallow river, William had no choice but to play a waiting game. He and his brothers kept the *Mary Ann*'s hold full of trade goods and supplies and prepared for departure as soon as the waters rose.

Each morning William walked down to the riverbank to examine the marker he had installed to monitor river levels. Every morning he felt a hollow sense of disappointment fill his chest. Even a ride up to Gumeracha, an afternoon spent walking with Bessie and a couple of nights at Kenton Park, the family home, failed to raise his spirits.

Months passed. April, May, June, and July. The river dropped so low that it would be impassable to a rowing skiff. William's ambitions seemed churlish and irresponsible, and his father began to make noises about recalling all of his sons to Gumeracha.

Through these soulless days, news of Captain Cadell and his progress came constantly, for the big-city press loved to record the Scotsman's movements. The fitting out of the *Lady Augusta* was soon completed, followed by her departure from Sydney under the command of Captain

Davidson. The newspapers reported the *Lady Augusta*'s arrival in Melbourne, and didn't they crow when Cadell himself met his creation at Port Elliot, taking command for the run through the Murray river bar!

The time advantage that the Randells had enjoyed was being frittered away to nothing.

CHAPTER ELEVEN

Cadell and the Bar Crossing

BEFORE ME LIES almost half a mile of breaking waves, dangerous waters indeed, even for a man who has sailed from the age of fourteen, and conquered river bars all over the world. I am a seaman second to none, but even I feel the cold breath of fear at bringing the *Lady Augusta* through the Murray mouth, and over the bar, for if she should founder every penny I own will founder with her.

If I shall cross, good things will come my way. Governor Young and his pandering government are in my pocket, and all I have to do is bring this vessel through, then beat that damned William Randell and his brothers to navigate the river.

'Stand away,' I shout from my place at the helm. After twenty-four hours of lying at anchor in five fathoms, waiting for the seas to calm, I will wait no longer, and we circle again, still building steam and power in port and starboard engines.

This Murray River bar of South Australia is the worst I

have seen, for of course I have been capsized in a small boat here in the past. Today I will overcome My pride as a seaman, and a Scot, will not allow me to fail here, though the vessel beneath me is not a sea boat, but a paddle steamer, made for rivers. She is one hundred and five feet from stem to stern, and twelve feet across the beam – yet without the depth of keel to track her straight, and with the windage of her multiple cabins causing her to scud sideways with every gust.

Ahead I see the western and eastern shoals that guard the Murray's mouth, then the broad gape in between. Much of it is shallows, but the men I landed on a beach inside the estuary some months ago marked a narrow channel through. I can see the buoys now, between the backs of the rollers crashing in, even as we aim for the throat of the channel.

At the last moment I turn full lock and we bear away out to sea again. One more circuit, hoping for a lull. My heart is hammering. The bar is dangerous, but I must get through, today, and it must be now, at the full flood tide, for during the ebb the bar is impassable.

Finally, is it a lull? I glance behind and the next few swells are indeed a little smaller. I swing the vessel around, and point her again at the gap.

'Do we have full steam, Mister Napier,' I call, addressing the engineer.

'Yes Captain.'

'Then hold hard, we are going through.'

With both engines at three-quarter speed, I take the *Lady Augusta* into the channel, feeling that unearthly swoop as the powerful rollers take the ship in their grip. Yet ahead the surf is confused, and a sideways wave smashes us on the starboard beam. My stomach lurches as we ship water: tons of water, the free-surface effect heeling the boat sharply from one side then another. Everything I own is at stake here. Each plank of the *Lady Augusta* is hocked to the last nail.

Holding the wheel hard to port the hull straightens, though an increase in speed makes us plough into the back of the wave I am following. The one behind breaks onto the stern, and I hear the shouts of my crew, as I focus on bringing us up and on.

I ease back on the regulator – waiting, waiting – then open up again to full speed. We surge onwards, with both paddlewheels thrashing us forward, now finally finding position in clean water between two waves. The key to a following sea, as every good mariner knows, is to choose a wave and match its speed, sitting just behind the shoulder, never allowing its predecessor to catch up, nor to let your vessel reach it.

'We're going to make it,' shouts my chief officer, a Yankee named Copeland, his accent twanging over the sounds of wave and sea, 'Good going skipper.'

Another wave: another series of swells and breaking white water, and then abruptly we are through and into the relative calm beyond, with Mundoo Island ahead and

Hindmarsh to port. The crew cheer and raise their hats, someone starts singing Rule Britannia and I let them have their moment, trying not show my own relief.

'By God Commander,' says Davidson, clapping his hand on the small of my back. 'You must have iced water in your veins.'

I turn to him. We have a plethora of captains aboard. Davidson had skippered the *Lady Augusta* on much of the sea journey from Sydney, and will take over again while we steam up the river. Edmund Robertson, also on board, will captain the soon-to-be-launched barge *Eureka*, while I serve as Commander of this fleet of two boats, which will give me sufficient time to ingratiate myself with my passengers and ensure the flow of funds.

'Enough chatter,' says I. 'We shipped water, get those pumps working. You'll take command as soon as we reach Goolwa.'

'Very good sir,' says Davidson and I can tell by the spring in his step that he is pleased at the prospect, as any good leader would be.

CHAPTER TWELVE

The Dry River

WHEN CAPTAIN CADELL pushed through the river bar to the relative calm of the Goolwa Channel, the Randell brothers had suffered through months of waiting for the low and sluggish Murray River to rise. Yet this was no ordinary surfeit of rain, it was a long and terrible dry that became known as the 'Black Thursday' drought of the early 'fifties.

Day after day, the waters fell further, until the marker itself was high and dry, and recording the drop became pointless. Word came that the Darling had become a chain of pools filled with floating dead fish – no longer flowing at all – and apparently getting a rowboat through the Murrumbidgee from Wagga Wagga to Narrandera was nigh on impossible.

With the spectre of Cadell on their tails, the Randell brothers waited for a fresh in the river, and the work of improving and fine-tuning the *Mary Ann* palled on William. Worse still, his father was not prepared to have his sons spend their time in unprofitable activity. It was a bitter blow when Elliot was recalled to the farm to tend the orchards. If all this wasn't enough, the three-hundred-pound cheque that had been promised from the South Australian government – money that William needed desperately to show his father that their efforts were showing some return – had not arrived, and appeared to have been forgotten.

With each new snippet of news William fell deeper into a sense of despondency that only another visit to Gumeracha to see his family and Bessie could lift him from.

It was a cool mid-August day when he spent much of the afternoon walking with Bessie through the crackling-dry paddocks of Kenton Villa, across the road from the Randell's property, talking of very little, but feeling warm in his heart from every glance and the exchange of some of their very first loving words.

Bessie, at seventeen, was a sensible, attractive and lively young woman. Her face, surrounded by curls, was both determined and full of fun. When they held hands her skin was cool and dry. William had a feeling that anything was possible when he was with her.

His mood improved immeasurably over that very pleasant hour, though this was not to last. Having said his farewells, he was heading home through the Nickels' front garden when he was hailed by Bessie's mother, who had been pruning roses.

Elizabeth Nickels Senior, like a good proportion of Gumerachans including the Randells, hailed from Devonshire and spoke with a strong accent. She had the same name as her daughter, but a rather different demeanour. Secateurs in one hand, and a thorny length of rose stalk in the other, Mrs Nickels confronted William across a garden bed fringed with local stone, her stubborn chin out-thrust like a weapon.

'Excuse us, William Randell,' she said.

'Yes, Mrs Nickels?' He paused, hands in his pockets, impatient to get across the road to a warm kitchen and a cup of tea.

'Well I just want to tell ee that you're paying a little too much mind to young Bessie, and I, fer one, am not thinkin' on marryin' her off to a bey near twice 'er age.'

'Not twice 'er age,' complained William. 'I'm only twenty-nine.'

Elizabeth held her ground stubbornly. 'Too much difference fer my liking,' she said, 'an' I won't have it. Cast yer eye somewhere else, for that's a union that won't proceed while I live to ferbid it.'

William stared at her, heart sinking, then turned on his heel, wondering when anything was going to go right for him.

The next morning, as he prepared to leave, William found a gift-wrapped package atop his saddle, which was sitting on a beam that served as a rack in the stables. A card affixed by a ribbon said, 'From Bessie to William. Not to be opened until you reach the Darling River!' Smiling again, William carefully stowed the gift in his bedroll.

In no hurry to get back to Noa No, William walked his horse all day, then camped beside the track near Blumberg – a spot the brothers favoured because of a tiny spring and a flat clearing. He had scarcely set off after breakfast the next day when he saw Tom riding towards him at a canter, his horse near blown, horse and rider sweating even in the cool morning.

'What is it?' cried William, expecting the worst.

Tom's face was animated, almost bright red. 'It's the bloody river – she's rising. Twelve inches overnight, and more even while I saddled me horse – I've got the boys warming the boiler now.'

There was no need to say any more, for William was already digging his heels in, and his gelding responded, eager for the run. By the time they reached the river at Noa No the measuring stick was reading almost forty inches and still rising.

'This is no flash in the pan,' said William. 'We can steam as far up as we've a mind to this time.'

'And we've still got the jump on Cadell by a few days,' agreed Tom.

'We leave this very day,' roared William. And while the holds were already full of trade goods such as tea, flour and sugar, and the fuel holds were bulging with three-foot lengths of red gum log, there were a hundred final tasks that needed to be done. All the Noa No farmhands were called to the fray, and human chains passed goods into the *Mary Ann*, floating free and able to be brought up higher and closer than ever before.

The boiler was blowing off steam, and they were just about to cast off, when the rapid hoofbeat of a lone horseman sounded from further up the lane towards Mannum. William paused from being about to climb aboard for the last time, watching the man come. He was riding too fast for his ability. He was tall and gangly, a little awkward in his seat.

The horseman stopped beside them and swung off his horse, and William cried, 'Why, it's the Reverend Davies. What are you doing here?'

The newcomer was pink-faced from exertion, around William's age, eyes shining with excitement. 'I was in Mannum, and saw that the river was on the way up. I heard the Lord God in my ears, and He spoke to me. He told me to ride and beg that you will allow me to journey upriver with you.'

'We'd be honoured,' said William, figuring that having one of Heaven's earthly representatives on their side could only help matters. 'You only just made it, we're about to cast off. There may be hardships. Can you manage?'

'With the Lord's help, I can,' said the Reverend.

William turned to one of the crew. 'Quick, help the Reverend Davies get his gear aboard.'

Finally, a little after one in the afternoon, with just that small group of farm workers to clap them off, the *Mary Ann*'s paddle wheels began to churn, and away she went into the fast-flowing river. The Reverend John Davies was good company, delighting in every aspect of the scene, pointing out this and that on the banks and speaking of natural beauty and its creator as one and the same thing.

William was ecstatic but also sad. Leaving Bessie had been difficult, but his thoughts now roamed over fractured ground. She was still a child. Her mother would never let them marry. They would have to be just friends, the very best of friends. But how could he be happy if she married someone else?

His mind touched on the gift-wrapped package that he was not to open until they reached the Darling. It was now nestled in his kitbag. For that, as much as any reason, he wished to reach the Darling River as fast as the *Mary Ann* would carry him.

CHAPTER THIRTEEN

Anne Francis Finniss

WHILE THE RANDELL brothers and their crew began their second attempt to steam up the Murray from Noa No, the dignitaries invited to take passage on the *Lady Augusta* began to make their way towards Goolwa.

One of these privileged few, Mrs Anne Finniss, waited until the footman had opened the carriage door, then climbed through, settled back onto the leather seat and arranged her skirts. Her good friend Mrs Irvine, then young Louisa Younghusband followed, the former removing her gloves and the latter, just eight years old, putting on lady-like airs that made Anne smile. Her own son Travers, of course, had insisted on sitting up on the box next to the driver and he was already asking questions and pleading for a turn at the reins.

Anne was more than a little surprised at herself. After all, the idea of joining the 'first' (for so the Governor and his staff kept repeating as if the Randell brothers did not exist) steam-powered voyage up the Murray seemed to be not only adventurous, but also a little frivolous for a mother and hostess.

Captain Cadell himself had invited fourteen-year-old Travers to come along on the voyage. Anne and her husband, Colonial Secretary Boyle Finniss could hardly let him go alone, yet would they deny the boy the trip of a lifetime? Boyle would be busy administering the colony whilst the Governor, Sir Henry Young, was also on the voyage, and thus Anne agreed to go.

Strangely, Anne didn't find the prospect of a five-week adventure altogether distasteful. She, like most of South Australian society, admired Captain Cadell very much. This realisation had at first made her feel guilty, before she decided that it was not sinful for a strong-minded woman to think well of a man other than her husband, provided it was purely in a theoretical way.

Anne, and the other ladies who moved in Adelaide's highest circles, knew themselves to be members of a new breed of woman – independent, not subject to the social mores of England. Anne, although she had married an Englishman, would always be proud Irish, true to her County Westmeath roots, and originally of a social class far below that of Mrs Irvine, Mrs Young, Mrs Palmer and the others.

Anne was also something else that these ladies were not. She was a genuine, twenty-four-carat beauty. Even at sixteen years of age one glance of her face had compelled Boyle Finniss, then a Lieutenant of the 82nd Regiment, stationed in the town of Mullingar, Ireland, to pursue her from the moment he laid eyes on her.

When Anne insisted that she would not marry a soldier, Finniss sold his commission and applied for a land grant in Australia. Originally landing in New South Wales, Finniss had sensed opportunity in South Australia and moved the young family there.

Now, at thirty-four years of age, Anne's skin was clear and healthy, her hair shining auburn, and she had the defined jaw and strong cheekbones that artists loved to paint. Her years were hard-earned, with six living children and one deceased, yet the active Irish girl was still inside her – the spirit of adventure and love of new horizons. Again, the excitement at spending many weeks aboard a boat with Captain Cadell rose, and she subdued it. Her husband was a good man – honest beyond reproach and with all the virtues – thinking of other men did not become her.

That night the carriage stopped at Alexander Anderson's Emu Inn at Morphett Vale, and Travers, just fourteen years old, treated Anne as if he was her escort. He was a sturdy boy, with the intelligence and honesty of his father, and a smiling face.

It was quite a party that night at the inn's dining room, enjoying the hospitality of their Irish host, and passengers from a second carriage – the Younghusband family including their three daughters, along with dignitaries Mr Bright and Mr Palmer.

'All these girls,' Anne quipped to Travers when they reached their room. 'You won't know which one to flirt with.'

'Shush mother, I've got better things to do than fret about girls.'

The next day a couple of incidents broke the monotony of travel in light but persistent rain: once when one of the horses drawing the lead carriage fell over on a steep and slippery slope, and the other when a tree branch caught the canopy of the second. Both times Travers went to help. Just fourteen-and-a-half, he was already such a fine young man that Anne's heart almost burst with pride.

Arriving at the Goolwa at last they craned their necks looking the *Lady Augusta* moored in the river. Anne did not see her as an ugly boat, but a new kind of vessel, made expressly for the interior waterways of her adopted country.

As they left the carriages, Captain Cadell came ashore to greet his guests, and there was a spark in his eye as he kissed Anne's gloved hand. A boat was prepared to row out with most of their luggage, and a tour followed. This began with the steamer, followed by a stint aboard the new barge, the *Eureka*, which was to be launched the following day.

A tented camp for the official party had been prepared just out of town, and after the tour Anne and the others embarked again on their carriages. As they pulled away from the riverbank Anne looked back and saw Captain

Cadell in animated conversation with a dark-haired young woman – very pretty, with the gloss of youth in her eyes.

'That's Miss Williams,' said Mrs Irvine. 'The one who will launch the *Eureka* tomorrow – just as she did the *Lady Augusta* in Sydney.'

'She's very attractive,' said Anne.

'Yes,' said Mrs Irvine. 'Strange that Captain Cadell would bring her all this way just to launch a barge.' She pursed her lips and lowered her voice so Louisa Younghusband would not hear. 'Though of course he may not have brought her all this way for that reason only.' There was a strange expression in her eyes, as if she were watching Anne's face for a reaction.

CHAPTER FOURTEEN

Launching the *Eureka*

ANNE FINNISS, her son Travers, and the other guests camped in field tents belonging to the 11th Regiment of Foot, the British garrison then stationed in the colony of South Australia. These had been made more habitable with stretcher beds off the ground and warm blankets. One tent had been outfitted with a cast iron bath. In a clearing near the river a warm fire had been lit, and after supper the company gravitated to chairs arranged around the blaze.

The gentlemen began to tell stories, an activity greatly enlivened when Captain Cadell himself arrived in a whaleboat with his captains, Davidson and Robertson. Miss Williams accompanied the group also, dressed demurely in Indian muslin and a grey woollen cloak, sitting quietly to Cadell's right side, making little eye contact and appearing to Anne's eye at least, to be distinctly unsettled.

There, around the hearth, Anne watched her son Travers hero-worship Cadell, as the young sea-captain told stories to fire a boy's imagination. He told how at Travers's own age of fourteen he had signed on as a midshipman on the *Minerva*, an East Indiaman of almost a thousand tons and one of the greatest trading ships afloat. He told of daily life on board as one of the ship's most junior officers, on the 'Great Circle' route through the Indian Ocean.

He told stories of being hoodwinked by a Portuguese trader in Macao, of the pagodas in Canton, and double-dealing Chinese officials. There was scarcely a sound as he related his rapid promotion – fifth officer by the age of eighteen, and then his part in the Opium Wars between Great Britain and China, beginning with the requisitioning of the *Minerva* as a troop ship and ending with the bloody siege of Ting-hai.

Cadell told the enraptured audience of cannons with mouths wide as a man's spread arms, of gunshot wounds and raw naked terror and Anne felt herself melt with admiration, knowing that she was not the only woman there who was deep in his thrall, the soft Scots tones of his voice working together with the sounds of the river and the night creatures.

'I was third officer of the troopship *Eruaad*, at the end of the war,' said Cadell, 'and by then I was grown up indeed. Graduate of a hard school, I might add.'

He told of his promotion to first lieutenant, at which point he was given an incorrect navigational order by the captain that he refused to obey, believing that it would result in the destruction of the ship. 'I lost my position,' he said. 'But I saved the lives of a hundred men in so doing.'

He locked his eyes on young Travers. 'So do you know what I did then?'

The boy slowly shook his head. 'No sir, I do not.'

Cadell grinned wolfishly. 'I was given my own command and spent twelve months hunting the blood-thirsty pirates of the Malacca Strait. In appreciation of my efforts, I was given a sword by the Sultan Zainal Rashid Al-Mu'adzam Shah I of Kedah. It's in my cabin in the *Esmerelda*, and I'll show it to you the first chance I get.'

When Anne looked at Travers, his eyes shone, in rapture at the possibilities painted in the air by a skilled storyteller who did not shrink from placing himself as the centre of the action.

Near midnight, at the change of the tide, Cadell rose to his feet. He announced that he would head off back to his berth on the *Lady Augusta*, and finished with a rough schedule for the following day. The company rose and applauded, shouting 'hear, hear,' as the Scotsman and his entourage walked back to their boat, and rowed away with the current.

Preparations for the launch of the barge *Eureka*, arranged for one pm the following day, took most of the morning, with the women busy bathing, doing each other's hair, and dressing in finery brought for the occasion. Only Mrs Younghusband had brought a maid to assist her, and Anne detested this need with a silent passion.

Travelling by carriage to the Goolwa jetty, they found it

crowded with onlookers: locals and tourists from as far away as Adelaide. Anne and Travers were in time for the Governor, Sir Henry Edward Fox Young's arrival, announced with the firing of cannons and musketry.

Miss Williams was there also, in an ostentatious blue satin dress with so many layers of petticoats so that it flared out from her tiny waist like the sails of a clipper.

The band had hardly finished their first tune when Captain Cadell mounted a dais and announced that the launch would not proceed until the following day due to a technical problem with the *Eureka*. There was a stunned silence, and Anne gripped her son's hand, sensing his disappointment.

More disappointment and ill-luck dogged the launch. The following day the event was again scheduled for one pm, and a slightly smaller crowd gathered. The band was still enthusiastically present. Captain Cadell, as he had the day before, mounted the dais and regrettably announced that the launch was again not possible.

Anne happened to be very close when Miss Williams turned on Cadell and hissed. 'You are making a fool of me. You've dragged me halfway around the country, for what?' She threw down the scissors that would have cut the silk sash. 'I will thank you to have my things collected, and find a coachman to take me to Adelaide, for I will not tarry here another day.'

Two days later, at eight in the morning, the barge *Eureka* was finally launched. Her decks had been garlanded with banksia flowers and in the absence of Miss Williams, Lillie Younghusband, just thirteen years old and smiling like a doll with this great honour, cut the ribbon to a chorus of shouts and cheers.

All that day men laboured to load and prepare the *Lady Augusta* for departure. Anne settled into the ladies' quarters on board, and she and Travers partook of the feast planned for that day. The not-quite finished Goolwa Hotel was still a couple of months away from opening but her staff prepared yet another feast of Herculean proportions, and the diners were entertained by a member of the crew singing a bevy of colonial songs, *Come, Fill the Flowing Bowl* and *Hurrah for a Bushman's Life*. Anne thought that his voice was average, but his efforts pleased her nonetheless.

It was seven in the evening when the *Lady Augusta*'s steam was up and she powered into the stream with the barge *Eureka* lashed to her starboard side, the departure bell ringing and a band of crew members on the deck playing *Off she Goes*.

The few words that Anne knew rang in her head as the musicians played, a fiddle taking the lead.

Off she goes to Donnybrook Fair,

She's got time and money to spare,

Looks like rain but she don't care,

Off she goes to Donnybrook Fair,

Then they called out 'Three cheers for Captain Cadell, and the first steamer on the Murray,' followed by a bellow of 'Huzzah!'

Even Anne knew that the *Mary Ann* was already one hundred and fifty miles upriver, having sailed a few days earlier. The official line, it seemed, was that the other paddle steamer was just some kind of experiment and didn't really count. Captain Cadell, they reasoned, would swiftly overhaul it. Anne, like everyone else on board the *Lady Augusta*, believed that he would.

CHAPTER FIFTEEN

That Cursed Boiler

WILLIAM RANDELL had enjoyed a challenge since the day of his birth. He was thirteen years old when his parents left their hometown of Kenton in Devonshire, and boarded the *Hartley* for a sea journey across ten thousand miles of ocean to Australia. Life on board a three-masted sailing ship was tough, and the *Hartley* was just ninety feet long with a beam of twenty-three.

After five long months of storm seas, stagnant calms, hunger and disease, the Randell family stepped ashore at Port Adelaide, South Australia, the latter being an institution that was younger than William. It was, however, a place of opportunity – the first Australian settlement to be gazetted as a province rather than a colony.

After years of hard work, with the Randell family both contributing mightily and at the same time benefiting from the brisk pace of settlement, William was quietly furious that the government had turned their back on he and his brothers. He was also missing Bessie, and her mother's warning not to pursue the relationship was flying in the face of a stubborn desire to spend every possible moment with her for the rest of his days.

In that first week of steaming up the Murray there were too many incidents to allow William to fixate excessively on love and anger. The main problem was boiler leakage, caused partly by poor design, and partly the departure of Elliott at their father's orders. The younger brother had learned to gentle the boiler along. He knew just how much heat it would stand; when to rake or spread the fire and when to blow off steam.

The new 'engineer' had no such skills. He was a blunt, unimaginative kind of fellow, a hard worker, yet unable to anticipate just how much heat 'one or two more' red gum logs would produce. The bullock chains they had wrapped around the shell were holding, though frequent stops were required to remove blackened and weakened wooden wedges, then create new ones to drive in and tighten the chains further.

'That cursed boiler,' came the shout, over and over, when it hissed and steamed, and the paddlewheels lost impetus. The sound of a sledgehammer pounding against a new wedge would follow and finally the stoker or deckie would shout that power had been restored.

All in all, these were days of frustration, made worse by a following breeze from the south that captured emissions from the stack and shrouded the *Mary Ann* with smoke. The only positive was that the sail could be unfurled and their forward motion assisted.

On a positive note, the Reverend John Lloyd Davies turned out to be great company. He was a schoolmaster as well as a man of religion, and he had an interest in, and some knowledge of, almost everything. No cod or callop would be caught without him dissecting its innards, exclaiming at the shape of the heart, or evidence of its diet that he extracted from slimy strings of gut. Davies also loved to sing, and his tenor voice boomed out across the waters at odd moments, competing with the racket of the steam engine, occasionally joined by Tom. He made notes and sketches and threw himself into the adventure of that journey with great spirit. Groups of Meru on the banks or navigating their bark watercraft were of special interest. He called to them as the *Mary Ann* passed, and carried on a barter when he could.

Finally, working on a strict protocol of steaming only during the day and tying up to a tree branch overnight – often lighting a fire and carrying sleeping gear ashore, they navigated the Big Bend for the second time. By Saturday of the first week, they had limped their way ten miles above Moorundie, a busy depot town in those days. There William decreed that they would spend the Sabbath in a state of rest. He was pleased at having a minister aboard to deliver the service.

'We shall,' he proclaimed, in a theatrical manner, 'awaken the echoes of this river's primeval solitudes by the voice of prayer and the song of praise.'

The Reverend John Davies conducted the service very early the following morning, while steam rose from the water. It was a beautiful moment, with the sun rising over the trees that crowded the banks, giving both the verge grasses and the river waters a yellow glow, while a cold wind stirred from the north-west.

When it was over William requested one last prayer.

'And what would that be?' asked Davies.

'Could we pray that God will help us to reach the Darling Junction before that devil Captain Cadell?'

'Of course,' said Davies with a malicious grin, and again they bowed their heads.

The following day the *Mary Ann* finally steamed to within sight of the spot where they'd been defeated, back in March, by shallow water and mud-bars.

'It's just ahead Will,' cried Tom.

'What is?'

'That shallow place where we turned back last time.'

William's hand whitened on the tiller. His nervousness, however, was unfounded. Deploying a lead line, they consistently sounded between twenty and thirty feet of water depth, and there were smiles all round. At least the river was now on their side, and they were learning to live with the boiler.

'Full ahead,' he shouted, 'nothing will stop us now.' Inside William's mind, however, he intoned one more prayer, this time asking for Heavenly assistance in ensuring that the worst of the boiler problems were behind them.

CHAPTER SIXTEEN

Up the Goolwa

THE FAILED LAUNCHES of the last few days are an embarrassment and disappointment to me, but now, as we pull away from the Goolwa jetty with the barge *Eureka* lashed alongside, I am satisfied that my reputation is intact. The empty space in my bed where Miss Williams, until recently, has slept, is a lack I feel keenly. On the other hand, her presence on board and in my cabin would have been a scandal and she is not the kind of woman easily hidden. Her departure, on balance, is for the best, and when I set both engines for one-quarter revolutions, heading upstream in the Goolwa Channel of the Murray River, she is the last thing from my mind.

Rather, my thoughts concern only the river herself and the safe navigation in the dark of this glassy evening. My boat, the *Lady Augusta*, so homely and box-like from a distance becomes beautiful to those on board. She has luxury berths for twelve gentlemen forward, and four ladies aft, as well as my own cabin, sleeping accommodation for lesser guests and my officers, as well as hammocks for the crew below decks. She is fully 105 feet in length, her upper works of New Zealand pine, as are those of the *Eureka*, with a hull of blue-gum planks. She smells of tar and wood, fresh from the adze. Lanterns burn aft and on the hurricane deck, and her stacks stab towards the sky where the glow of stars make such a brilliant array that the dignitaries arrayed on our decks point and exclaim at their beauty.

A huge fire is burning on the bank, a column of sparks rising in a line upwards into the firmament. All day the Ngarrindjeri people – those dark-skinned fishers of the lower river lands – have been gathering in numbers, piling up firewood. They were given two sheep which they suspended above the flames and have now cut down to eat. I see their figures in the firelight, dancing with bloody chunks of mutton-flesh in their hands. I hear the tapping of sticks and the drone of otherworldly instruments that fade with the increasing revolutions of the engines.

The jetties and the fire are soon past, and our little quarterdeck relaxes somewhat, able to fixate on the route, and I tell my captains and lieutenants that they best get used to travelling by night, for I will not allow the Randell boys in their home-made paddle steamer to reach the Darling Junction before me.

Yet I feel strangely breathless and alone. I realise that I am afraid. Yes, I have faced Chinese guns, and the very worst Atlantic Ocean storms, where a ship becomes a helpless lump of flotsam. Yet, I am afraid that the *Lady Augusta* will strike a snag missed by the lookouts and sink with loss of life. That one of the foolish lubbers cavorting on the deck will fall overboard and drown themselves. There are so many ways in which my plans can go awry, and I must control my fear that they will come to pass.

That first evening, however, is like a dream – passengers climbing the ladder to thank me for bringing them on this journey. All are in an excellent mood with the assistance of fine champagne. They can see now that the *Lady Augusta* and her barge are well suited to this river work, and the Russell and Company engines are truly excellent – of the latest compound horizontal type, smooth and quiet, and the chuff of steam with each cycle is comforting, the boilers holding their pressure at a consumption of just four hundred pounds of wood per hour.

In three hours of night-steaming we run fifteen solid miles, almost to Lake Alexandrina, and there, in a broad segment of the channel we set a single anchor, and with a watch officer charged with keeping look-out and maintaining coals in the fireboxes, we go to our beds.

At four o'clock in the morning, after a light but refreshing sleep, I wake and accept hot shaving water from Jeray, a native of China who serves as both second steward, assistant to John McAulay, and my own personal batman. Dressed and presentable, I rap on the door of William Davidson, nominally the master of the *Lady Augusta*, but overshadowed, I know, by my presence on board. William Webb the Chief Officer and Napier the engineer share a cabin and I knock until I hear a reply.

'I want full steam by quarter-to-five, men,' I say, and I hear the groans, but they do not dare complain.

By half past four I am topsides, while Tom Nevin and Henry Petrie the Able Seamen prepare to raise the anchor. Firebox doors clang as the stokers Rob Robson, Evan Thomas, William Cruise Teague and Lewis Chandler bring up more three-foot lengths of red gum and stoke the fireboxes. By ten to five the anchor and hawser are stowed, and we are travelling at half revolutions up the channel, the gentle splashing of the paddlewheels bringing the scent of the river, not unpleasantly, to our nostrils.

As breakfast is served the vista of Mount Barker near the mouth provides a talking point for the guests. Water birds in vast numbers, tens of thousands perhaps, take to flight and blank out the sky with their wings. I see swans, ducks, signets, spoonbills and pelicans in uncountable numbers and I can only guess at the resources of small fish that must exist to sustain them.

As we prepare to round Point Sturt into Lake Alexandrina, an expanse of water some thirty-five miles by fifteen in size, Mr Davidson warns me that according to the port-side watch the south-westerly is blowing Force Six and I can feel how the wind works against the blunt sides of the *Lady Augusta*'s cabins.

'Should we lay up here for the day and hope it blows

itself out?' asks Davidson from his place beside me.

'No. We go on,' I say. 'But the crossing must be swift. Three quarter speed ahead now.' And under a blue sky buffeted by cold and inclement winds, we enter the broad expanse of Lake Alexandrina, and I can see how the breeze has whipped its surface into a frenzy, foam flecked on the surface and catching the sun.

The journey that has theretofore been smooth and pleasant, changes into a rampaging ride of troughs and crests as the shallow water and the wind increases to Force Seven, a near gale. Within an hour most of the guests are sick, and it is a terrible sight to see Mrs Younghusband bent over the rail. Again my fear returns. I need the goodwill of these people for my plans to come to fruition, and seasickness does not make for a kindly disposition. I pray that none of the gentlemen or women aboard demands to be returned to shore.

It is strange, but Anne Finniss, the wife of the Colonial Secretary, seems to be unaffected by the malaise. I watch her assist the other women, and her carriage remains upright and her colour strong. She is an exceedingly handsome woman, as the best of Irishwomen can be. I know about her humble but honest beginnings and admire her already. I am also fond of her son Travers.

Seeing the way that she weathers that lake crossing, I admire her a little more.

CHAPTER SEVENTEEN

The Swamp

ANNE HAD NOT failed to notice the flashing looks from Captain Cadell as the *Lady Augusta* tackled the lake, but she was determined to ignore him. In fact, with her son beside her, and after several hours of assisting ill passengers, the attention did not sit well with her. A sense of indignation began to grow.

Under no circumstances, she told herself, would she allow herself to be the subject of a shipboard obsession. As if to punctuate this emotion she glared from her position on the promenade deck to the wheelhouse, where Captain Cadell stood with his captains and happened to be looking her way. Anne's glance caught him by surprise, and he turned sharply.

Travers placed a hand on his mother's shoulder and leaned into the view of Pomanda Island. It was a strange but picturesque little place, surrounded by reeds and thickly colonised with shrubs. 'May I cross to the *Eureka* to help Captain Robertson?' he asked.

'Not in these conditions,' said Anne patiently. 'It might be dangerous. Soon enough we'll enter the river and things will calm down.' The lake had already begun to narrow as they approached the river entrance.

'So, I can go across when we enter the river?' he asked, as if determined to extract a formal promise.

'For sure you can,' she agreed, and reached up to touch his hand, just as Mr Mason, the South Australian 'Protector of Aborigines' came alongside. He was a man of medium height, with chocolate brown eyes and a fondness, Anne had earlier decided, for the sound of his own voice.

'Young Travers,' the gentleman said. 'You should be thankful we don't land at Point Pomond, for it is infested with snakes. There are hordes of the damned things.'

Anne shivered theatrically. 'Snakes? Well it's a good thing we're not stopping.'

'What kind are they?' asked Travers, his interest piqued. 'Blacks, tigers or browns?'

'Black snakes mostly, but some brown fellows as well. I've shot twenty of the vile creatures in a single day there.'

'You live near here, don't you Mr Mason?' Anne asked.

'Yes, not far ahead, on the reserve. Come with me to the other side and we'll be able to watch it coming up.'

Anne and Travers dutifully followed their guide to the starboard rail, which was already lined with spectators. Their height above the water provided a tremendous view on either side, and to Anne's eye the eastern bank appeared as flat meadows peppered with stately pines. The grass was very green near the river, with scattered cattle grazing.

'That land to starboard,' Mason went on, 'is Portalloch Station – belongs to a Scot called Neil Malcolm, and a good fellow he is too. The white house there is his, and that's him waving now.'

The lake was less than half a mile across by then, growing calmer by the yard, and ahead they saw the entrance to the Murray River itself, a moment of excitement for all the passengers. It was surprisingly narrow there, and murky with the earth of inland flood plains. Anne now gave Travers leave to skip over to the *Eureka*.

'Be careful,' she said, but he was already gone.

A mile inside the river, Mason pointed out a heap of cut wood stacked on the right-hand bank, next to a new jetty made of red gum piles and planked with the same timber. 'This is the Reserve coming up now,' he said. 'Our sable brethren have been cutting wood for some days for fuel. Rather excited about the whole thing they were, I must say.'

'You get on well with them, don't you?' Anne asked.

'I do. I've lived in the area now for more than a decade – I was a policeman at Wellington, so I'm pleased to say that I have their respect, and they get nothing but fair dealing from me. They are not all the same – being from different groups, with similar but discrete languages, but most of them identify as Ngarrindjeri.'

'Stand by all,' came the booming voice of Captain

Cadell. 'We will stop and load fuel here. You may step ashore briefly if you wish.'

The engines surged, belching smoke that filtered the sun brown as they swung into the new jetty. Now the paddles ceased their revolutions and the chief steward supervised the lowering of a gangplank, and the disembarkation of the ladies and gentlemen who wished to go ashore.

A swarm of black men, bearded and agile, appeared and began the work of loading the boat. Most wore ill-fitting European clothing, with a smattering of furs and more traditional garb. Members of their families were on the shore: mothers with babes, and small children running and smiling. Some of the women, Anne noted, were bare-breasted.

Travers appeared again, hurrying back from the *Eureka* to this new source of excitement, full of limitless energy. 'May I help with the loading, Mother?'

'I suppose it won't hurt,' she said, and she watched with pride as he ran over to join in the work, loading his sturdy arms as full as any grown man and bantering with the labouring Ngarrindjeri.

'He's a fine lad,' said Mason.

'Thank you. Boyle and I are quite proud of him of course.' She pointed across at a stone house in the distance. 'That's your house, is it?'

'Yes, that's it. I can see my wife coming along now. I'd best go and meet her.'

'You've done a good job here. These … Ngarrindjeri look remarkably healthy.'

'Thank you. The work of civilising and bringing Christianity to them is proceeding beyond expectations.'

Mason walked to the ladder, descended, and left the *Lady Augusta* via the gang plank. Anne saw how some of the labouring men called to him as he went, smiling and laughing. The Protector of Aborigines was popular with his charges, it seemed.

It was mid-afternoon when the *Lady Augusta* reached Wellington. A crowd had gathered in front of the Inn, shouting out their huzzahs as the paddle steamer hove into view. At that moment also, the government ferry had almost reached the western bank, loaded down with men, horses and equipment, all setting out for the goldfields.

Ashore, too, the gold-seekers were lined up, waiting to board when the ferry had disgorged its passengers, or were camping nearby, a few desperate returnees calling out the foolishness of those setting off.

'It aren't like what you think,' one dishevelled digger called. 'Don't believe what you hear – there aren't no nuggets layin' around waitin' to be picked up, and the likely ground is all pegged. If you don't 'ave capital don't bother.' A huddle formed around him, some incredulous, others downright aggressive towards him.

With some hours to kill, Travers first prevailed on Anne to buy him some shot and caps for the small-calibre revolver his father had allowed him to bring on the journey. Then, back on the steamer he disappeared again, weaving through the crowds of Wellington locals taking the opportunity to step aboard the first 'real' paddle steamer on the Murray.

A short time later he was back, his face shining with excitement, gripping Anne's hand excitedly, 'Mother, there's an interesting swamp across the river – full of water birds. Lillie Younghusband wants to go for a row, and Captain Cadell gave me permission to take one of the skiffs. Can I please?'

Anne smiled, 'I don't think it's seemly for you to head off on the river alone with Lillie.'

'Then you can come too, can't you?'

Anne had been looking forward to sitting down with her novel – she had lately been reading a book that all her friends were talking about – a spooky tale called Wuthering Heights by Emily Bronte. Yet, Travers was almost impossible to say no to – and that was part of what worried her about letting he and Lillie get away from adult eyes, across the river somewhere.

'Of course I'll come,' she said. 'Let me get my coat.'

Lillie Younghusband was such a lively young thing, dressed in a spotted dress and white bonnet, that Anne couldn't help getting caught up in the spirit of this adventure. Travers rowed like a man across the current and still had the wind to talk constantly. Anne remained in the background, occupying the bow seat, enjoying the excursion very much.

Across the river they found the entrance to the swamp, and it was true that the surface was alive with birds. Pelicans, ducks, black swans and a dozen other species took to noisy flight as the rowing skiff approached.

There were vast armies of reeds, and shallow places where the water was no more than waist deep, the tips of dying grasses still visible, having been inundated by the rising waters. Red gums and paper barks grew on islands and banks, often partially draped with green creepers. The trunks and limbs of dead trees rose in eerie grey shafts from the water.

For some thirty minutes Travers rowed, laughed and sky-larked, the two youngsters leaning over to splash each other or pointing to a blooming lily-flower and once, a black snake shimmying across the water surface. Anne, however, was growing conscious of the passing time. 'We really need to go,' she said. 'Captain Cadell will be wanting to leave.'

'Can I have a quick swim first?' Travers said.

Lillie burst into laughter, 'You're insane, Travers, it's the middle of winter.'

Anne inclined her head reluctantly, and Travers stood, stripped off his shirt, and dived over the side, surfacing a stone's throw sway from the boat, bursting through the surface and blowing a raspberry. 'It's cold alright,' he said, but made no move towards the boat. Instead he duck-dived down, returning with a handful of swamp detritus that he threw in Lillie's direction. It fell short, but it was enough to send her into fits of giggles.

Again Travers dived, and Anne waited for him to surface, but seconds ticked past. Her heart started to hammer uncomfortably. 'Travers?' she called.

A moment later the *Lady Augusta*'s steam whistle blew distantly. It was a recall. Anne looked around desperately. Travers had still not surfaced. Even Lillie had stopped laughing, and was looking desperately around them.

Anne stood up, heedless of the now rocking boat. Her voice rose in pitch and cracked out across the water. 'Travers, you get back here right now!'

Again the steam whistle sounded, and Lillie stood also, peering around at the water. All the humour and fun had gone from the day. Anne's voice thinned with the strain, and she saw that Lillie was close to tears. The mood had changed, just like that, and Anne tried to reason out how many seconds had passed since her son had gone under. The pain in her chest was like a knife, as again the whistle sounded.

A moment later Travers burst from the water, laughing. 'I bet I had you worried,' he gasped.

Anne's temper had always been quick to rise, and even with the relief that came flooding into her, she turned on him. 'You stupid boy. Get in this boat right now. Captain Cadell has been blowing the recall and if we are late I will die of embarrassment.'

Anne fitted the oars to the rowlocks while Travers sulkily climbed over the transom. He sat, shivering, his skin pale and covered in goosebumps, then raised himself to change places into the rowing position, but his mother was already beginning the first stroke.

'I'll row, you just get yourself warm,' she snapped.

'I didn't even know you could row,' he said miserably.

'I can do a lot of things you don't know about,' she said, and it was true, for she had grown up within a stone's throw of the River Bhrosnach, on a bend as it wound through Mullingar. Her childhood had been filled with boats and skipping stones and tickling trout from the water on river bends.

It was a good distance back to the *Lady Augusta*, but she rowed skilfully, and finally, when they came up to the steamer the engineer was blowing off steam and all other passengers had boarded. Captain Cadell said nothing as he watched Tom Nevin help them aboard, but his face was thunderous, and there were no more admiring glances that evening.

CHAPTER EIGHTEEN

Closing the Gap

THE MURRAY VALLEY had changed its character many times since the *Mary Ann* left her makeshift boatyard at Noa No. It was sometimes narrow – bounded by steep cliffs, and sometimes broad, with grassy floodplains stretching to distant hills. At times spectacular rock bars narrowed her width, or the high waters inundated lagoons as wide as lakes and thick with birds. The journey was slipping into a routine, with the stoker learning to 'baby' the boiler, and incidents had become less common.

Now, as William steered the game little steamer across a fast current near Paringa, the left-hand bank was gently sloping, well-grassed, and adorned with yellow flowers. On the right was a low knoll, and a cluster of buildings at its base.

'There,' cried William, pointing ahead to the left bank. 'John Chapman's station ahoy.'

'I see it now,' agreed Tom. 'And it looks like they're expecting us.'

This fact was obvious, for a flag was flying on a rough bush with an Irish phrase stitched onto the face, 'Céad míle fáilte.'

William turned to the Reverend Davies. 'Any idea what that means?'

'It means a "hundred t'ousand welcomes", to be sure,' said Davies, delivering an Irish brogue as if he was born to it, making the elder Randell brother smile. And as they neared the bank, John Chapman and a brace of his workers made up a greeting party, standing on the freshly sawn timbers. Behind them stood a vast mound of cut firewood. Seeing this, William frowned, for he could discern no reason for this stockpile. Still, there was much to do, making the paddle steamer fast to the bank.

William knew John Chapman by reputation only, but he liked the man straight off as he jumped over the gunnel and down to the boards to meet him. The station-owner was older by around ten years, with a weathered face, big hands, and a slow-talking manner that telegraphed honesty and good manners.

'I can't tell you how excited I am about the opening of the river to navigation,' Chapman said. 'We ran out of tea a week ago and the carriers aren't due with our next supply load for a month. The girls have been drying native mint leaves and brewing a cuppa from that out of desperation.'

'No more,' smiled Will. 'We've a good supply on board.'

As the deckhands assisted in unloading an agreed quantity of flour, tea, rice and tobacco, the rest of the party walked towards the homestead. On the way William asked Chapman about the pile of firewood. 'There must be ten ton at least. What's it all for?'

Chapman, in his straight-talking manner, did not try to avoid the question. 'Captain Cadell wrote to me a few weeks back. He asked if we'd cut and stack fifteen ton of fuel in three-foot cords. He offered a good price so I agreed. It seems that he's in a powerful hurry – I hear that he's nigh on reached Moorundie as we speak.'

William felt a jolt in his chest. 'I didn't realise that he was so close.'

'Travelling day and night, I hear,' said Chapman, 'by lantern light when he needs to. They say that he won't be slowed down by man or God.' He paused. 'From what I can work out he's just four days behind you, and closing the gap fast.'

'Looks like we'd better get a move on,' said William.

'I'd hate to see the damned Scot win,' said Chapman. 'Take what you want from the wood piles. My men will make it up before Cadell arrives.'

'That's a tempting offer, but I don't have much in the way of cash to pay you. I could let you have a little extra flour, but I need to establish the trade further upriver and show my father that the trip is worthwhile.'

'No charge,' said Chapman. 'As I said, take what you need.'

William inclined his head. 'In that case I can only say that today you have made yourself a friend and ally. One day, when Cadell has gone to some new challenge across the sea, I will be running a fleet of paddle steamers past this station. Your kindness will be repaid in ample measure.'

'It seems then,' smiled Chapman, 'that I have made a sound investment for the future.'

With the knowledge that Cadell was so close behind, William did not waste too much time on Chapman's tasty luncheon of roast hogget and sweet potatoes. By two they were engaged in loading not only cut wood, but fresh fruit and vegetables, and a keg of salted beef. By four, filled with that delightful sense of having sealed new friendships, the boiler was hot and the twin paddle wheels propelled them out into the stream.

'There's a good moon until at least midnight,' William declared. 'We'll get as far as we can. With the Scot on our tail we can't afford to relax.' But he was worried, for with two, sometimes three knots of river current now against them, they were barely making four knots of headway. Cadell's more powerful steamer would surely be doing better.

'How far to the Darling Junction?' asked Tom.

'A week, if that cursed boiler holds up, and we don't dawdle like we've been doing. We've three tons of wood on board, thanks to Mr Chapman, so that saves us half a day of hard work for a start.'

Tom had lately, now that they were away from their

father's disapproving eyes, taken to smoking a pipe, and this he produced now, thumbing some tobacco into the bowl and lighting up with a vesta struck on the bulkhead. Once it was drawing well he observed; 'Perhaps we should have thought of that – having piles of wood cut for us along the way.'

'It's a mindset thing, isn't it?' Davies asked. 'The famous Captain Cadell finds ways to get other men to serve him, whereas you Randells are a breed who likes to do things for themselves.'

'True words,' agreed William, spinning the wheel to avoid a deep snag, barely the tip emerging from the river just ahead. 'Yet, it always seems to be the other kind of man who builds empires.'

'That's not what you want from life, surely?' asked Davies.

'Not an empire, no. The kind of success Cadell wants is not what I aspire to. Given the opportunity, a man like him will subjugate and enslave. I'm more interested in building networks – a business based on trust and friendship like my father has done at Gumeracha. A man's kindness benefited us enormously today. Both of you surely know that his gift will be repaid many times over – and I will never forget.'

'Bravo,' applauded Tom. 'A man needs rules to live by, and I think that yours and mine are the same.'

'Each man,' said the Reverend Davies, 'acts according to his nature, but in some the capacity for empathy is buried deep. Bravo indeed, and the success you will no doubt find will be richly deserved.'

Running at night was strange but beautiful, with sparks flying heavenwards from the stack, and the shapes of migratory birds far above on their long journeys under the stars. It was a strangely calm evening, until an hour before moonset when the *Mary Ann* struck a hidden snag. This began with a thump, lifting the starboard bow to a frightening angle and causing shouts of consternation below.

William dropped the snuff box he had been holding in one hand, then heaved the tiller sharply to starboard, and cried, 'Shut off steam.' And almost as soon as the paddlewheels slowed, the hull came around, scraping along an underwater obstruction. William prayed silently that the pressure would not burst a seam or smash a timber.

It was all over in a moment, but William felt sick to his stomach. The most dangerous snags were hard enough to spot in the daytime, let alone in darkness. With the steamer dead in the water they opened hatches, leaning down with a lantern and checking for damage below the waterline.

'No damage at least,' Tom said at last, as they and the crew gathered on the open deck with a thin moon above, and the rhythmic heaving call of a tawny frogmouth coming from somewhere nearby on the bank.

'We survived that one by the skin of our teeth,' said William. 'That's it. I won't go another yard tonight. If the cost of beating Captain Cadell is a hole in the hull then it's not worth it.' He turned to the stoker. 'Close it down – just enough coals to keep it warm for a start at daybreak. We'll set off then like a scalded cat.'

Yet, even when he went to his bed, William could not sleep. The spectre of the *Lady Augusta*, with her decks crowded with dignitaries and sight-seers closing the gap was all too real in his mind.

CHAPTER NINETEEN

Tenbury

NAPIER, the *Lady Augusta*'s Chief Engineer, asks me for five hours of stopped engines to perform maintenance. I promise him three, and we set two anchors in the river mud off Moorundie and lie straight in the current. During this down-time, I send our guests ashore, cowering under umbrellas because of the drizzling rain.

This wasted time irks me, for I desire with all my heart to set off on those serpentine river bends, and on into the increasingly arid valley that contains the stream. My passion for catching and overtaking William Randell is consuming me. A disease for which only grinding the upstarts into second place is the cure.

It is a relief to see the passengers leave my sight and head ashore, out of my way for a period. I am happy to see them go. How tired I am of them all! Governor Young, and the dignitaries Kinloch, Grainger, Palmer and the rest. The wives and daughters are no better. They expected a picnic cruise in first class conditions, but their quarters are tight, the food is scarcely Ritz-standard and they are growing weary of the journey, despite having barely started. I am tired of their veiled complaints about the food, the sanitary arrangements, night travel, and constant requests to visit with station and farm owners along the banks, leading to interminable cups of tea in drawing rooms. I am even tired of Mrs Anne Finniss and her mixed signals.

I am tired of trying to impress the Governor and William Younghusband with my knowledge and abilities and I regret the scheme to bring them all along. I am tired of trying to keep young Travers Finniss away from Miss Lillie Younghusband for I know what a lad and lass of that age have on their minds and I want no such scandal on my command.

Now, at least, I have some respite, and I soon have the crew busy cleaning, coiling ropes and polishing brass work. I see that William Gylmore, the cook, has opened negotiations with some dark-skinned river people called Moorundie, who come alongside in their mongue watercraft, trading sticks of plug tobacco for fat cod.

The engine maintenance is a success, and I would have proceeded up the river again that instant but when the dignitaries return, they bring a man and two women of the Moorundie across in the skiff with them, treating the man with an indulgent patronage.

The man, Tenbury by name, is enormously tall, dark as night, with the bearing of a monarch, scarred across his chest and upper arms, his skin damp from the rain and his eyes dark incantations set deep in his skull.

Tenbury has apparently and visibly been shaved of every hair from his body and scalp with a stone blade, and Mason, who is known to him, explains that he is mourning the loss of a son, which is why he is in such a state.

Our impromptu guest, however, needs no interpreter. As well as his own Meru dialect, Tenbury speaks English with a wide vocabulary. He appears to understand the questions and comments of the passengers who, including the women, surround Tenbury and his two wives, all dressed regally in animal furs, and ask him inanities such as, 'How does one cook an entire wallaby?' or 'How did your people live without hospitals?'

At the conclusion of this salon of poor taste Tenbury pulls Mason, the Protector of Aborigines, who seems to be known to him, close and whispers something.

'Tenbury would like to sing us a blessing for our journey,' Mason announces.

'How perfectly wonderful,' says Mrs Irvine.

'A fabulous idea,' enjoins Mrs Younghusband. She turns, 'Louis, Lily, Sarah, come listen to Mr Tenbury's song.' Others gather too: Travers and his mother, and I feel the instant stress of her presence. Those of the crew who are not immediately engaged in work came also.

Tenbury draws a deep breath, then throws back his head, doing something strange with his eyes so that the whites take the place of his pupils. He begins to sing, low and dramatically. I know from the start that he is not singing us a gentle lullaby, and I can see from Sub-Protector Mason's face that he knows this too.

I know a curse when I hear one, and Tenbury's curse springs from deep down in his gut, and when his eyes return to their normal state the pupils never leave mine. When Mason, as if reading the anger in my eyes tries to stop the song short the ladies titter, but the dark man finishes with a glare of hatred so intense that even I stagger from the force of it.

I recover myself enough to say. 'We thank you for the blessing, but now we must be on our way.' I turn to the captain of the *Lady Augusta*. 'Clear the vessel for departure, Mr Davidson. We leave in ten minutes.'

And after two of the seamen have escorted Tenbury to the skiff, preparatory to rowing him away, Mrs Irvine says, 'What happened to the poor man's son?'

Mason does not answer, but walks away down the deck as if he has not heard.

Over the coming days, that encounter with Tenbury takes the swagger from my stride and causes me to feel pessimistic when I should be hopeful. I am angry that my passengers brought him on board for their amusement, heedless of the dangers that lurk behind his eyes.

Steaming on up the river, the next evening we load firewood, labouring well into the night, igniting a bonfire to light the loading parties as they carry armloads of fuel on board, and our guests, always anxious for diversion, make the bonfire their own.

I watch the work proceed, alone on the promenade deck, leaning against the rail when Anne Finniss ascends the ladder, taking her place beside me. The firelight touches the proud features of her face and I know that I have never seen a more beautiful woman.

'You do not seem to be yourself, these last few days,' she says. 'Is there a problem?'

'None whatsoever. Only the responsibilities of command. They can wear a man down, at times.'

To my vast surprise, the Colonial Secretary's lawful wedded wife slips one hand onto my back where it burns like fire. 'I've watched the way you run the ship, and I admire you very much.'

'Where is Travers?' I ask, somewhat lamely.

Anne chuckles, her hand still resting in the small of my back. 'At the bonfire of course, entertaining Lillie. Don't worry, Mrs Irvine is watching them.'

For a moment I let the gentle Irish lilt of her accent echo in my mind as if it is a sealed cave that might trap the cadence of her voice forever.

Such is that moment of rapture that I do not hear the sound of boots on the ladder, only a subtle cough behind us and I turn to see Davidson approach. Anne drops her arm like a gun and turns away without a word.

CHAPTER TWENTY

The Eccentric Wheel

LONG DAYS FOLLOWED, and Anne Finniss felt the tension on board the *Lady Augusta* more than most. Captain Cadell drove his crew and passengers to their limits, with the vessel barely at rest for three or four hours in the deepest hours of the morning. Anne noticed that even Arman, the smiling Madrassee deckhand, began to shuffle between his duties with his head down, and a melancholy cast to his face.

Anne's thoughts turned often to the romantic moment with Captain Cadell on the promenade deck. This had not been repeated, and they had scarcely spoken since. Their eyes, however, had delivered many a poetic line across the deck.

When the *Lady Augusta* did come to rest in the middle of some dark night, the deckhands were too exhausted to keep watch, and Travers was one of several younger passengers who had volunteered to take this duty on, so the seamen might snatch some sleep. Anne had argued against this, but made no headway against a fourteen-year-old desperate to prove his manhood.

Nothing terrible had happened. In fact, Travers had executed these night-watch duties with aplomb.

On the evening of the first of September, both passengers and crew were anxious for some respite by reaching John Chapman's station at Paringa.

Yet, early that evening, the *Lady Augusta* was inadvertently steered into an anabranch that appeared to be the main channel. She steamed on into this mistaken route for more than a mile before the leadsman reported that there was no longer enough depth to continue. A turn was begun – no easy task with a barge almost as large as the paddle-steamer lashed alongside. The anabranch, moreover, had become a narrow channel, studded with drowned trees. Soon afterwards the shouted voice of Captain Cadell reached every corner of the ship and barge, dressing down the officer-of-the-watch who had made the error.

This delay meant that the jetty at Paringa did not come into sight until after nine pm, In the darkness of the riverbank nearby a limp flag waved the same Irish greeting that William Randell had seen a few days earlier. The words took Anne back to her distant homeland: *Céad míle fáilte* – A hundred thousand welcomes.

With the *Lady Augusta* tied up to the bank Anne joined a party to head ashore to partake of station hospitality. At the same time shore-fires were again lit, in order to illuminate the work of taking on wood that Mr Chapman's men had cut for them. Anne and the party of dignitaries were given a sumptuous dinner, their numbers swollen with local squatters and Mr EB Scott, the sub-protector of Aborigines.

Also, at the station that night, they found a police constable waiting in an out-building with a chained Aboriginal prisoner: one of several who had killed two white men on their way from the Darling. The other offenders had been shot trying to escape.

After dinner, before returning to the *Lady Augusta*, Mr Scott took the company out to view the prisoner and his captor. 'If you could carry him to Wentworth for trial I'd be much obliged. He needs no shelter, just a shackling-point for his chains, and the scantiest of rations.'

The prisoner was taken on board by the constable and two armed station-hands. Anne watched with fascinated horror from the promenade deck as the latter fastened his prisoner to the rail aft, while the constable sat nearby with a rifle on his lap.

'I for one, dislike having a killer aboard,' Mrs Irvine declared. 'What if he escapes and goes on a rampage? I shall not feel safe in my bed – it was hardly fair of Mr Scott to make such an imposition on us.'

Anne did not reply, but she felt the same. And with the fires burning on the shore and the tramping feet of men finishing loading the holds with timber for the ravenous fireboxes of the two great engines that drove the *Lady Augusta* onwards, she went to her bed, but lay awake, filled with a sense of dread.

It worried her that Travers was staying up again to take watch, especially with the constable and his prisoner on deck. Lying in her bed, with the other female passengers snoring in their bunks it was all she could do not to get up and check on him.

Hours of short naps and wakeful interludes passed, and it was still very dark when she heard the stokers back at work, then finally the engines starting. The splash of the paddle wheels and hiss of steam was almost soothing, covering all other sounds. She saw the first light of dawn filtering in, then heard some of the others getting up and dressing for breakfast.

Finally now, Anne relaxed enough to sleep, and she drifted off again. She was in a heavy slumber when there was a terrible scream that carried through that boat like a knife through flesh, then the immediate stoppage of engines and the sounds of shouting.

Anne had dressed and reached the deck when they carried Captain Davidson up from the starboard engine room, screaming in agony, his leg foreshortened and the end mashed to a bloody pulp. At first Anne worried that the prisoner on board had gone on a violent rampage, but it quickly became obvious that an accident of a grievous nature had occurred.

Cadell fixed on the spectators and growled, 'Please,

everyone go up to the promenade deck and give us room to take this man to his cabin.'

There, up high above the river, Anne took Travers's arm. His face was white, shocked at what he had seen. Louisa Younghusband was crying, sobbing against her mother's leg

George Palmer, who had been helping in the engine room, had witnessed the accident, and now he held court on the facts of the matter. People, in general, listened to Palmer, for he was a Lieutenant Colonel himself, one of the founders of the City of Adelaide, and a comrade of Colonel Light.

Palmer smoked his pipe furiously, while his words came in staccato bursts. 'Davidson was walking past the starboard engine ... the boat must have lurched against a snag ... for it moved a little. Davidson, lost his balance for a moment ... his foot touched the eccentric wheel of the steam engine where it was grabbed and crushed to a pulp.'

'A terrible thing,' muttered Governor Young.

Palmer had not finished. 'No seaman would allow himself to fall victim to an accident like that unless he was tired beyond bearing; being driven by Cadell twenty-four hours of the day.'

One of the men said, 'Come on old chap, you can't lay the blame for this on our Commander?'

There was no answer but for the cawing of a crow in a river red gum and the sound of Cadell's feet on the ladder as he came up to reassure his passengers.

Later, Anne, like most of the other guests, visited briefly with the injured man in his cabin. He had been dosed with laudanum, and looked quite peaceful. Afterwards, passing Cadell's cabin she heard two voices inside. One was the American, John Copeland, Chief Officer of the *Eureka*.

'No one else will say what needs to be said,' came Copeland's New York drawl. 'This man needs urgent medical help, and we need to turn around and give it to him.'

There was a long silence, then Cadell's voice, 'Mister Copeland, I am the Commander of this voyage, and I will not turn back. Davidson must take his chances. There is a doctor at Wentworth, on the Darling, and we will proceed there with all possible speed.'

'From all reports Doctor Fletcher at Wentworth is long-retired – a simple landholder now. There is no hospital or infirmary there. For the sake of this man's health we should turn back.'

Cadell's voice cracked like a whip. 'We will not turn back, and you must say no more on the subject.'

Silence followed, and Anne walked away, taking care that her feet made no sound.

CHAPTER TWENTY-ONE

The Darling Junction/Bessie's Gift

WILLIAM RANDELL still preferred not to steam at night, and as August moved into September the longer days made that dangerous practice unnecessary. Rising at four, the *Mary Ann*'s crew built the fire methodically, introducing heat to the still-warm boiler as fast as they dared. Most mornings the boiler was blowing off steam when the first reflections of dawn glimmered on the river surface, and the piston moved in the jacketed cylinder, imparting motion to the beam.

Accompanied by a huff of steam being expelled through the vents, the beam's longitudinal motion ended in a cam, providing rotary power to the twin paddle wheels. It was always a moment of relief to William, when the paddle wheels turned for the first time, dripping with river water, and within three or four revolutions the *Mary Ann*'s hull overcame her inertia and began to move.

Over those next few days, at the tiller with a strong mug of tea, William steered the game little steamer on a general easterly heading, passing out of South Australia. From then on Victoria claimed one bank and New South Wales the other. They made good time, apart from occasional stops to cut fuel, or when the boiler needed cooling – it still leaked if the stoker allowed the firebox to burn too hot.

The Murray Valley, in the last few days, had grown more arid. The banks were still lined with stately river red gums, but immediately behind it stretched plains of saltbush and bluebush, along with Mallee trees.

On the morning of Saturday, September the third, William gave the tiller to Tom while he consulted his charts – sketches really, based on the movements of explorers and travellers – annotated with snippets of information heard in river inns and from the local people of the river. A moment later he looked up at his brother and grinned. 'I don't believe that we can be more than a mile from the Darling.'

'Really, that close?'

'I'm certain of it. We're going to beat that bastard Cadell!'

'Well done to us then,' said Tom. He pointed ahead at the river surface, 'And look how the colour of the stream changes from the left bank to right! The Darling waters aren't mixed in yet. We're close, and no mistake.' And he called for Davies to join them on this historic occasion.

The three men were together when they rounded a bend, and up ahead they saw a narrow, wooded isthmus in the middle of the stream, and a yellow-brown channel on the left.

'The Darling,' shouted William.

Reverend Davies let out a whoop, then a shout of praise.

A deep excitement pervaded William's chest. Not only because they had beaten Cadell to this spot, but that they had done something historic. Also, there was a package in his little cabin, that gift from Bessie that said on the card, *Not to be opened until you reach the Darling River.*

Tonight, he would open it.

William brought the *Mary Ann* in to the bank at McLeod's Crossing, the little settlement just inside the Darling's mouth. He and Tom did a roaring trade selling flour, outside the Inn, and squatters rode in from miles around to toast the voyagers and inquire of cartage prices. Others wanted to view the steamer and her engine.

There were wild bush characters of all kinds at the Inn, and the Randell party took it in turns to keep watch on board the *Mary Ann*. They were taking no chances with theft or worse.

In any case, William had no intention of remaining in the Darling for long. By late afternoon they threw off the lines and motored back downstream, around the long sweep of the junction, and back into the Murray.

'So we've beaten the famous Captain Cadell to the Darling,' said Tom. 'What's the next challenge?'

'He's not far behind us,' said William. 'It would be a

shame to let him beat us to Swan Hill. I'd like to get another ten miles behind us before we stop for the night.'

After supper, long after they had tied up to a snag for the night, William took the package from his desk drawer. The gift had been sealed in a biscuit tin, and he grasped the lower section in his right arm, with the nails of his left hooked under the lid while applying a gentle, steady pressure. The lid soon parted from the bottom of the tin.

Inside, amongst a slight smell of must, the gift itself was wrapped in gold paper. Inside he found a card no bigger than the Queen of Hearts, the front illustrated with one of Bessie's own honest watercolour scenes of tawny-yellow hills and sharp gullies.

Laying the card down, he opened the rest of the package. He found a gold frame, and inside it a daguerreotype of Bessie herself. William exhaled slowly. In the last few years he had seen only a very few daguerreotypes – a very new technology. It was akin to magic, as if she were suddenly there with him. It would have been expensive and difficult for her to have obtained the image – there were several practitioners of the photographic art in Adelaide, but she would have had to travel to their studio and sit still while the machine did its work.

William continued to stare at the image for some minutes. Nothing else but this young woman seemed important now, not even having beaten Cadell to the

Darling; not opening up the river trade, not impressing on the South Australian authorities that a few brothers from the Adelaide Hills could build a river steamer from scratch that could trade the length of a nation's mightiest river.

As William opened the card a lock of hair fell out, and he squeezed it between thumb and forefinger, feeling the clean texture of the fibres. Three words fell from his lips, 'Oh, dear Bessie.'

The card's interior was filled with words in neat and small script.

> Dearest William
>
> By now you will be riding at anchor in the far-away Darling River, and your achievements, brave and well-deserved, will be a matter for history books.
>
> Lest I have become vague in your memory, I enclose a likeness of myself and a lock of hair to remind you.
>
> I look forward to the day when we can be together in the kind of companionship I hope and pray for.
>
> Forever yours
>
> Bessie

William could scarcely believe it. This was as good as a declaration from the woman he loved. She was telling him that in spite of her mother's feelings they would be together. They had a future.

He raised the lock of hair delicately to his nostrils and inhaled. Some vestige of her scent must have remained, for it triggered strong emotions in his heart, and brought tears to his eyes.

At that moment William knew what he must do when they returned to Gumeracha, that quiet place in the Adelaide Hills. His future was on the river, but he could not tame it alone. Only one woman in the world could possibly take her place beside him, and somehow, her mother had to be brought around to accept him.

CHAPTER TWENTY-TWO

Fever

THE MANGLING of Davidson's foot gives me the excuse I need – to steam onwards in the *Lady Augusta* without suffering criticisms of burning out the crew or putting the safety of the ship's company at risk. The injured man's wound is infected, which appears to have caused a fever to spread through his body. The calls to turn back grow fainter, for we are past the point of no return. Doctor Fletcher at McLeod's Crossing on the Darling is Davidson's only hope.

As we steam on towards the Darling, I hope to see the *Mary Ann* hove-to around a bend somewhere, struggling with the boiler troubles I have heard so much about. This dream does not come to pass, and I have to face the fact that the Randell boys have beaten me to the Darling. This race, however is not done – they had many days start on me. On the next leg of the journey our relative positions will be more even.

There are other problems, of course, to take my

attention. One of these concerns two young passengers. I remember myself how fresh blood sings in the veins in the summer of youth. Two days out from the Darling I come around the main cabin and stumble upon Travers Finniss and Lillie Younghusband in a fierce embrace, their lips pressed hard together.

This means trouble. Both are the offspring of men whose positions are tremendously important to my ambitions. In addition, the mothers of both youngsters seem to be distinctly cool to each other. I can envision the Battle of Waterloo if the young lovers are caught, especially if kisses lead to the touch of hands in more sensitive places.

William Younghusband is my agent, and a strong source of goodwill and funds. Finniss is the Colonial Secretary and a powerful man. I cannot allow my ambitions to be threatened by amorous youngsters. I withdraw from the scene, but wait until I find young Travis alone while the boilers are being replenished the following day. He is on the *Eureka*, with a fishing line trailed over the stern, leaning on the taff rail like an old hand.

'Now listen young Travers,' I say. 'This situation with you and Lillie Younghusband must stop.'

He looks up at me, a worried crease in his eyes. I feel a little cruel, for I know that he hero-worships me. 'What do you mean, sir?'

'You may look, you may talk, but you must not touch. Do you understand me?'

I watch his adam's apple rise from his collar. 'Yes I do,

sir. I understand.'

'Look. Talk. Not touch,' I repeat.

This time he merely nods, but his face is stricken, probably worried that I will tell his mother. This I have no intention of doing just yet. As I make my way back to the helm of the *Lady Augusta* I cross the path of that very woman, the beautiful Anne Finniss. I redden with the thought that my own advice to Travers, might equally apply to myself.

'It looks like Randell has beaten us to the Darling,' said Mason the following night, cruising in darkness along the right-hand bank. It is late – after eleven o'clock, but I will not stop this night until we reach the Darling. We have already passed the mouth of that river's main anabranch, late in the afternoon, and the excitement amongst our guests is at fever pitch.

'Yes, it looks that way, I admit. But he won't be far ahead, and this isn't over yet.'

Just a mile before we reach the Darling, we see a fire burning on the bank ahead, spilling its light out into the night, so it seems as if the river itself is aflame. Beside it are the shirtless people of the river, growing excitable as they see us approach.

With our guests arrayed on the promenade deck to stare, three of the fire-side people set out in their mongue from the bank and head towards us. I can make out two men and a woman. In a moment I realise what might happen now.

'Full stop,' I shout, and I hear the answering cries of Napier the engineer, and the clanging of metal; a change in engine beat and the abrupt cessation of both port and starboard wheels. Even so, it is too late, and our bow wave catches the mongue, and swamps their boat.

We pull two males from the river, but the woman swims ashore, as graceful as an otter on the Firth of Forth. The men too, can swim as well as fish, but are not quite as afraid of us as she. They stare around the boat with wide eyes, and make excited conversation with each other. One talks in shouted phrases with the prisoner still chained to the deck rail and bound for the Darling though I know not what they say.

In broken English they assure me that the Darling River is less than a mile ahead. With no time to help salvage the mongue we edge them back to the bank and leave them to their fire.

Finally, oh historic day, we enter the Darling. We can see the lights of the Inn. It is too late to send men to fetch Dr Fletcher, for his station is some miles from the junction. Horses will need to be borrowed, and Davidson will just have to last until dawn.

Yet, at least we can disembark the policeman and his prisoner, who has been such a malevolent presence. Relieved of their presence, I drop into a dreamless sleep, disturbed only by Davidson's fever-ridden shouts from his cabin.

In the morning we send a rider for Dr Fletcher, leaving Davidson in his hands and we steam on towards Swan Hill, some three-hundred-and-fifty river miles to the south-east. We are tired, the crew is strained. The passengers are squabbling and again I catch Travers Finniss amongst the cargo on the *Eureka*, in close embrace with Lillie Younghusband.

I exchange terse words with young Travers, yet that very night, I allow the boy's mother to massage my shoulders, aching from hours of command. This moment of weakness angers me, and I am abrupt as I walk away.

We forge on, past acres of reed beds, endless river red gums and the welcoming committees of river stations, the local inhabitants in their canoes and new horizons. My appreciation of the vastness of this land grows. Day and night we travel, and finally, finally, the moment I have waited for arrives.

CHAPTER TWENTY-THREE

Challenge at the Murrumbidgee

THE *MARY ANN* and her crew were tied up to a tree and settled into the late evening hour. William, Tom and the Reverend Davies were drinking tea on the foredeck. The crew were sleeping ashore, lit by the glow of a campfire.

It was a day to celebrate, for they had passed the junction of the Murray and Murrumbidgee – that third great Australian river that forms the Murray. This mighty waterway was spawned in the peat and marshes of the Fiery Ranges north of Kiandra, picked up the flows of the Queanbeyan, Goodradigbee, Yass and Tumut Rivers, the Crookwell and Abercrombie, and wound through snag-lined channels for nine hundred miles.

One day, William vowed, he would explore the Murrumbidgee, but for now the Murray was still yet to be conquered. 'Just three days to Swan Hill from here,' said William proudly, 'and us with a couple of tons of flour still to sell. The townsfolk will be pleased to see us no doubt.'

He raised his head abruptly. There was a noise from

downriver, something unexpected and loud, a cacophony of splashing, huffing and moving iron parts. A squad of flying foxes in the trees nearby left their perches with screeches of alarm.

'What in the name of the dear Lord is that?' breathed Davies.

Finally the *Lady Augusta* came around the bend – impossibly large, with a lantern mounted at the bow, surrounded by reflectors that lit up a good portion of the river. Covered paddlewheels churned away on either side.

Voices rising over the sound of the engines hailed them, and the engines slowed. A man appeared, leaning against the upper deck rail. William had never met Captain Cadell, but this surely had to be him.

'You took yer time to join us,' William shouted across. 'We reached the Darlin' three days ago, and well before you.'

'So what?' said Cadell. 'There was never any race to get there, for neither of us have a boat that qualifies for the prize money. The last leg was null, for you had a head start. The race is between you and me. From here to Swan Hill, and may the best man win.'

'Since when has the race been to Swan Hill?' spat William.

'Since right now. Take up the challenger or ignore it.'

And with these words, Cadell turned away from the rail. After a series of shouted orders, the paddlewheels started again, bearing the big steamer and her barge off into the night. William tossed the last of his tea over the rail. 'That, dear friends, was an insult if ever I've heard one, an' I'll be damned if that floating circus'll get to Swan Hill before us.'

'If we keep the boiler warm we can be underway at first light,' said Tom.

'No, we'll get underway as soon as we get the men aboard and we have steam to drive us. You know I don't like steaming at night, but this is different. All hands,' he called, 'get up and ready.'

Within an hour of that unexpected visit, the *Mary Ann* was tackling the first of the hairpin bends upstream of the Murrumbidgee junction, in pursuit of the *Lady Augusta*. Progress was, by necessity, slow, and William issued orders that the firebox should be kept aglow but not afire, with one of the deckhands sleeping while the other worked a four-hour shift, alternating through the night; bringing in wood, emptying the ashpan and giving the engine enough steam to keep up a steady three knots against the current.

'We'll take turns also,' said William to Tom. 'You go get some sleep and I'll wake you around three.'

'Are you sure you want to do this?' asked his younger brother.

'Of course I am. We didn't steam all this way to be taught a lesson by an arrogant Scotsman. We'll come to no harm if we keep our speed down, and it's a clear night with a good moon.'

The Reverend Davies remained at the tiller,

uncharacteristically quiet, while William peered ahead at the river, standing on the bench for better height, his night vision slowly improving as time went on, better on some headings than others as the river swung in its wayward angles. The banks here were heavily forested in places, but there were also long claypans near the shore that glowed white in the moonlight.

'You'd better get some sleep too,' William said to the Reverend Davies. 'I'll be fine here – it's quite peaceful at these low speeds.'

'Oh,' said Davies. 'I feel wide awake at the moment, but I'll head down when that changes.' He paused to clear his throat. 'It's interesting that after we hit that snag back in South Australia you said that you wouldn't steam at night again. What changed your mind about that? The river is even narrower here. Was it really that careless challenge from a grown man who should know better? You beat Cadell to the Darling – he refuses to accept that loss so now he's invented a whole new race to his advantage.'

William knew that every word was true. He hadn't wanted to navigate in the dark again, but Cadell had filled him with a burning rage – one that he could not seem to control – the desire to beat the Scotsman to Swan Hill now filled his soul so completely that even the thought of Bessie waiting for him back in Gumeracha faded out of immediate thought.

'What is it about Cadell,' the Reverend Davies continued, 'that vexes you so?'

William took a deep breath of the river-scented air through his nose, considering the question. 'I think it's because even though we're all newcomers to this country, my family and I have made a commitment to the place. We believe in building a future. Cadell is here only for himself – he craves the admiration of others, money, and influence. I care for none of those things.' He smiled, 'Well maybe a little, but not on the same scale.'

'Cadell is a big talker,' said Davies. 'But no one can deny that he's an able navigator and clever ship's captain. There's a place for people like that in the world.'

'That may be,' grinned William. 'But I wish that his place wasn't right here.'

Long after midnight, Davies did retire to his cabin, and William, alone and weary, was soon in danger of falling asleep. When his snuff box was empty, unable to head below to his cabin to refill it, he resorted to singing to himself very softly in the back of his throat, reciting poetry, and building dreams of the future – all based on good business practice and friendship – always on the waters and banks of this Murray River that he loved.

Three o'clock came around, and by then the mist had broadened over the river, so that from the foredeck William was peering down out into a mystic second river of white suspended over the first one of flowing water. The tips of some snags could be seen emanating from that ghostly mass, others remained beneath.

It was almost three-thirty, and William could not keep

his eyes open, when he brought the *Mary Ann* to a stop and woke Tom. He spent another ten minutes watching his brother handle their proud creation through the still-thickening mist.

'Promise me that if you have any problems or sight the *Lady Augusta* you'll wake me up.'

'That I will, and likewise if we end up hard against some dirty great snag.'

'In that case, I won't need any help to wake up.'

For less than three hours, William slept like the dead, and it was the Reverend Davies who shook him awake. 'You'll be pleased to know that we've caught Cadell and his crew napping. We're just about to pass.'

With a surge of excited adrenaline, William emerged to a brilliant dawn – with reds, purples and mauves in the sky, and the fog still hanging above the river. Water thrown from the paddlewheels also steamed a little, shrouding the afterdecks. Up ahead, the *Lady Augusta* and her barge were indeed at anchor. Her twin stacks emitted a grey smoke that indicated that she was in the process of heating her boilers.

'Good work, brother,' William said to Tom, and he called to the stoker to blow a cheery blast on the steam whistle. This had the effect of bringing guests and crew of both the *Lady Augusta* and the *Eureka* out on deck where they stared unhappily at the gallant little *Mary Ann*, that had bested them on a night-time run.

'By Heavens that is an ugly boat,' breathed Tom.

'You're right there, but she's got two very modern engines, and now we are ahead again we're going to be flat-out staying here.'

CHAPTER TWENTY-FOUR

Neck and Neck to the Wakool

LIKE MOST of the passengers on board the *Lady Augusta*, Anne Finniss decided that the prospect of a race was a fine thing, and when the *Mary Ann* churned past them at dawn, a gust of excitement blew through the guests. The last few days had been interesting enough already. Captain Cadell had wakened the ships' company at four am the previous morning to view a comet and its bright tail streaking across the sky. There had also been the introduction of dancing on the promenade deck after supper.

'How in deuces did Randell manage to get past us?' asked Governor Young, but Cadell was not on hand to answer, for he was already shouting orders, preparing to lift the anchors before the boilers reached full steam.

It was only when the *Lady Augusta* began chuffing upriver in close pursuit of her rival that Cadell shouted back from the helm station to the promenade deck, his voice fuelled with bravado. 'Ladies and gentlemen, we have a race on our hands.'

Anne admired Cadell so much at that moment. He was so full of confidence, obviously relishing the challenge, but soon he was lost to sight as he went about the business of commanding the boat. For the next ten minutes Anne stood at the rail, half listening to Jamieson and Bright discussing the relative power and speeds of the two vessels.

'The little *Mary Ann* has just one-fifth of our horsepower,' said Jamieson, 'but of course she's not towing a barge.'

'Exactly,' replied Bright. 'Her power-to-weight is possibly higher than ours, and she doesn't have the windage.'

'That boiler though ... everyone knows it's Randell's Achilles' heel.'

Travers appeared, his face shining with excitement. 'I can't wait to see the look on Captain Randell's face when we catch up to them. Mister McAulay says that we might even ram them – he says that Captain Randell is angry enough to.'

Anne ruffled his hair, 'Nonsense, the Chief Steward is getting carried away with himself. No one will be ramming anyone. It's just two captains having fun, that's all.'

'I saw a sea eagle nest on a tree on the Victorian side just before, did you see it?'

Before Anne had a chance to answer, Lillie Younghusband came up the ladder, and Anne saw her son's attention wander, hurrying over to whisper something in the girl's ear. Lillie giggled and they ran together down to the main deck.

As the morning wore on, the general interest in catching up to the *Mary Ann* grew to fever pitch. Soon the rival steamer was visible ahead on the longer river straights, and her nimble hull was proving to be faster than anyone had expected.

The *Lady Augusta* had an insatiable need for wood, however, and at Nurang, a station owned by a Mr Hamilton, they stopped and loaded a cache of many tons, which had been organised by letter weeks earlier, and cut by station workers. The loading was done at break-neck pace, and not even the most social of the ladies insisted on stopping for morning tea or luncheon.

Further on, at Cuttnab they found the *Mary Ann* at anchor, for this was a dairy station, and supplies of buttermilk, butter and cheese were welcomed by the crews of both vessels, and reason enough for a cessation of hostilities. The *Lady Augusta* anchored ahead of her rival, and reciprocal visits followed.

William Randell, his brother Tom, the Reverend Davies and a crewman came aboard the *Lady Augusta* for a tour, and Anne liked them as people but as rivals to her Captain Cadell's plans to dominate the river she despised them. Randell, to her, was a small man standing in the way of a big man, a sprat that was detracting from the glory of this first great river journey.

When a reciprocal visit was arranged, Anne demurred, but took a nap in the women's cabin, only removing herself when she heard the *Mary Ann*'s engines start. She emerged on deck in time to see the smaller steamer pass by, while Cadell finalised the stowing of goods and the readiness of passengers. The social visits, it seemed, had only intensified the passions of the two captains to race as far as Swan Hill.

Slowly, through the afternoon, the *Lady Augusta* crept up on the smaller steamer, until they could see her up ahead, her stack trailing smoke, on all but the sharpest bends. No one remained below by then, and Anne's hands gripped the rail, unable to understand why this race was suddenly so important to her.

The promenade deck was packed with guests craning their necks and exchanging encouragement – watching the river for a wide enough stretch for their captain to make his move. A cheer rang out as they came up near the right-hand bank, slowly starting to pull ahead. They could all see William Randell at the tiller, giving them a disconsolate wave and his gloomy expression provoking laughter from the *Lady Augusta*'s guests.

As they moved into the lead position Captain Cadell's voice rang out, rich with excitement. 'We have again snatched first place, Ladies and Gentlemen.'

For the next hour the *Mary Ann* pressed closely from behind. The wind had shifted, blowing strongly downriver, and the *Lady Augusta*, with her towering accommodations, caught the wind like a racing yacht's spinnaker. The smaller vessel was unburdened by the drag and windage of a much larger hull, and a hundred-foot-long barge.

There was suddenly a flurry of activity at the helm, and Anne soon saw the reason for this. A junction appeared ahead, and the left branch of the river looked to be of greater stateliness and width. It was obvious that there was a moment of indecision, a flurry of looking at charts, and shouted orders.

Finally the order rang out to steer for the left branch, and indeed it seemed to be the greater of the two. Again the engine beat quickened, and the paddlewheels churned the river surface to white. The decision to take that branch appeared to be borne out when the *Mary Ann* followed.

Yet, before long the direction of travel seemed to the more learned of the passengers to be incorrect, and even the less well informed began to mutter that their captain had made a mistake. The mood changed to despair when the captain of the *Mary Ann* backed up and disappeared towards the junction.

It seemed inconceivable to Anne that Captain Cadell had made a mistake, but worse was to come. A vast river red gum on the right-hand bank had a branch that grew out over the river, a stately and massive shaft of hardwood, and they could all see that the *Lady Augusta* was about to pass underneath.

With a shouted roar Captain Cadell ordered the engines into reverse, and the top deck cleared. There was no order in the confusion, and no time to carry it out, for that mighty branch swept the boat, and many of the passengers fell flat on their faces – ladies and gentlemen alike.

Anne was one of the first to regain her feet, and when the Captain called back to ask if there were any injuries it was she who replied in the negative. By then he was already engrossed in the task of turning the unwieldy vessel back the way they had come.

By the time the turn had been managed, and the *Lady Augusta* was steaming back towards the Murray, Jeray and Gylmore were already cleaning up a mess of leaves, sticks and gum nuts – and the passengers were back at the rail. Word arrived in the form of William Webb, the First Officer, that the channel they had just entered was called the Wakool, an anabranch of the Edward, and Captain Cadell had steamed into it purposefully, to discover its suitability for navigation. It was not, as some people might suppose, a mistake of navigation.

Any bad feelings or worry from this incident were dispelled when, a little down the channel, they came upon William Randell and his crew in the process of effecting repairs, for the *Mary Ann* had also had a run-in with an overhanging branch, and theirs had carried their mast clean away.

'See you at Swan Hill,' shouted one of the gentlemen from the rail, and even Anne felt as if the natural order of things had been restored, with the *Lady Augusta* in the lead. Life, it seemed to her, was suddenly very interesting indeed.

CHAPTER TWENTY-FIVE

Tangled in the Trees

I, CAPTAIN FRANCIS WILLIAM CADELL relieve the officer-of-the-watch and assume personal command of the *Lady Augusta*. After the time-consuming excursion up the Wakool, I waste scarcely a minute to hail the wallowing *Mary Ann* and her crew. There is a race I must win, and if affixing the mast takes them time, them that is all to my advantage.

We steam around the little paddle steamer and back into the Murray, yet the mighty river has narrowed, now choked with snags and overhanging tree branches. Even so, in an effort to put some distance between us and the *Mary Ann*, I order three-quarter revolutions in both engines. Beyond this speed our consumption of fuel grows prodigiously, and I do not plan to take on wood again 'til the race is run.

It seemed to me that we left the *Mary Ann* battling a serious position with the loss of her mast, but before we can begin to relax, within a mile in fact, she is behind us, with the mast in place, jury-rigged with ropes. On the next bend, refusing to slow, and forced to evade a snag, we are swept from bow to stern by another of those obstreperous overhanging trees. I hear and feel in my gut the sound of tearing metal. I shout for men with boat-poles, oars, anything, to fend the branches away, but much of the ornamental work on the first funnel and some deck furniture is carried away.

The *Eureka* fares even worse, with part of the handrail flattened, and a broken tiller wheel. My face is filled with the blood of my shame and frustration. This river is not so easy to tame, and I knew it from the start.

Meanwhile the *Mary Ann* comes alongside, and in an echo of our own actions a half-hour earlier, hails us with an insincere offer of assistance that I refuse forthwith, and deciding that any damage can wait, I use every man on board to help fend us away from the trees and back into the stream. Meanwhile, William Randell makes way upstream, ahead of us, with all the speed he can manage.

Again, we chase down our rival with everything we have even as a saffron-yellow sunset fills the sky and river with colour as if it were all of the same element.

Thirty minutes of growing darkness follows before we again have the *Mary Ann* in our sights. Now she travels slowly, lacking the lantern headlight that we use to illuminate the river on these long night runs. On a rare, wide stretch we pass her, our passengers who have imbibed on strong spirits and champagne jeering and cat-calling as we do so.

We steam on until exhaustion overtakes us. We strike overhanging trees again and again, and run hard against snags twice. The passengers are beginning to mutter about the wisdom of this night run. We anchor in the stream on a narrow point, effectively blocking any chance of the *Mary Ann* passing by us in the night, and I fall into my cabin bed to sleep.

My repose is interrupted by a pounding on the door, and the moment I come awake I can feel the issue. The boat is listing heavily, leaning at an angle so my cabin floor is at thirty degrees.

I hurry to my feet and find the First Officer, William Webb at the door. 'Sir, the boat is listing.'

'I can see that,' I snap. 'Do we have a damage report? Are the pumps working?'

'Not yet sir.'

'Well do it, and hurry.'

All the passengers are out on deck, complaining and howling like wild creatures. I select Petrie and Robson from amongst the gathering crew and send them below with a lantern. They are back in moments with news that the bilges are filled with water, causing the list to the port side.

Fortunately now, the pumps too are working, and a bucket chain established. Within an hour the water has been largely evacuated and the carpenter, Winsby and his mate McGregor are investigating several sprung planks, assuring me that we will be ready to steam on by sunrise.

With the crisis over, and the *Lady Augusta* again on an even keel, I go to my cabin. I hear a strangely gentle knock on the door. This is unusual, and I open it wide, staring at the apparition that stands before me.

It is Anne Finniss, looking more beautiful than Aphrodite, dressed in her night gown and robe. 'I can see that you're upset, about what happened,' she says. 'It's not your fault.' She reaches for my hand. 'I thought you might need comfort.'

I harden my heart. I want her more than anything, but taking the wife of the South Australian Colonial Secretary to my bed, on a crowded vessel, with all her cabin-mates knowing that she is not where she is supposed to be, would destroy my ambitions in an instant.

'Get out,' I hiss at her. 'Please, just get out of my cabin now.'

CHAPTER TWENTY-SIX

Swan Hill

WILLIAM RANDELL gripped the crosscut saw handle and plied it backwards and forwards smoothly over the thick river red gum branch, letting the sharp teeth do their work. Cutting dry wood for the *Mary Ann*'s firebox was a routine that both his mind and body had become attuned to – all in a day's work for the captain of a river steamer.

With each pass of the saw the teeth cut deeper, and soon the cord dropped, an exact three-foot length of nature's perfect fuel. Tom, on the other side of the saw, lifted the implement, chest rising and falling, while William measured the next length. Meanwhile, the Reverend Davies and the two crewmen laboured at filling the hold as quickly as possible.

It was scarcely dawn, and *Mary Ann* had been steaming or fuelling since not long after two am, with some urgency about the need to take on wood. The previous afternoon they had stopped briefly at a station called Pyangill, where they were warned that for most of the final twenty-five miles to Swan Hill, there would be no riverside trees at all, and fuel would become almost impossible to obtain. They had thus been forced to take on wood before they had planned to.

'Hold almost full sir,' shouted the stoker.

William stopped sawing to call back. 'Give us full steam in the boiler then please, and we'll be on our way.'

Together, William and Tom finished the cut, then helped gather the last armloads before clambering aboard for the final leg.

'All alert please,' called William. 'We have a race to win.'

Steaming on up the river, they soon came across the *Lady Augusta*, snugged in close to the left-hand bank. It took William a moment to work out exactly what was happening, for he could see daylight between the paddle steamer and her barge *Eureka* for the first time.

'They're letting the *Eureka* go – leaving her here,' said William. 'Damn.'

'Why is that a problem?' asked the Reverend Davies.

'Speed. Without the barge's drag she'll make three or four extra knots, and be twice as manoeuvrable.'

In the ensuing hours William found that reports on the nature of the landscape up ahead had been timely. Soon there was scarcely a tree to be seen on either bank. The full river had, in places, spread out across the floodplain, with acres of reed beds like the river Nile, and millions of ducks, geese and avocets taking to flight as the *Mary Ann* puffed closer.

The river channel itself was plagued with hard clay reefs that formed bulwarks against the current, visible in restive water movements on the surface. William inched their speed up as far as the weak boiler allowed, avoiding the outside of the bends where the current was strongest, and using the strategy of coming up under the approaching point, steaming straight across the current and up the opposite side.

'If only there was so few snags all along the Murray's length,' Tom said, but William was craning his neck, looking rearwards for the *Lady Augusta*.

Before half a mile had passed, the *Lady Augusta* was riding in the surface foam of the *Mary Ann*'s wake, looking for an opportunity to come alongside.

William yelled back to the stoker. 'Take the boiler up to thirty psi.'

'But sir, that might split her.'

'If it does we'll fix her, but I want to get to Swan Hill before that damned Scotsman.'

'Orright skipper,' came the call from below.

The Reverend Davies was looking quizzically at William. 'Is it really that important?'

'Yes. No.' William grinned. 'I don't know why it is. You think I'm being juvenile, but I would like to win this little contest.' He didn't try to explain that this was a struggle between the hard-working Randell brothers with a dream, against a blow-in who had managed to rally most of South Australia's aristocracy and all of the government to his flag.

'Even if we blow up the boiler?' Davies pushed.

'We'll try not to, of course,' said William, but his fingers tapped nervously on the wheel, and he had a panicky feeling in his chest.

Davies looked searchingly to where the strangely oblong-shaped boiler was venting through every seam and rivet, despite the bullock-chains that they had, weeks earlier, wound and tightened around the casing in order to keep her plates more or less intact. 'There's more steam getting out than going into the engine right now.'

'Bleed off a tad,' cried William, but in such a wide reach of the river it was becoming difficult for the *Mary Ann* to match the much more powerful and now unencumbered *Lady Augusta*. The larger steamer edged out until they were side-by-side. Every living soul on deck of the bigger craft was on the promenade deck, cheering and jeering.

For one or two minutes the contest was undecided. Port and starboard paddlewheels on both vessels were churning the river to froth, and the stacks streaming heavy smoke mingled with vented steam in their wake. The vertical beam of the *Mary Ann*'s engine was rising and falling faster than it had been designed to move.

For one moment it seemed that heart and effort would be enough, that the *Mary Ann* would hold her own against the twin horizontal engines of the *Lady Augusta*. A light head wind was favouring the smaller vessel, for the windage of the larger craft was enormous.

Yet, the *Mary Ann*'s boiler was spraying out steam in all directions, and this was not lost on the crowd of dignitaries and blue-bloods on the other boat. They began to laugh and point, and even Cadell appeared at the port-side rail to observe the near-disastrous venting with a grin.

By degrees, agonisingly slowly, the *Mary Ann* began to fall back, though she struggled on gamely as the *Lady Augusta* drew ten, fifty, a hundred then two hundred yards ahead. It was only when the bigger vessel had disappeared around a bend that William finally recognised defeat.

'Vent steam and spread the coals,' he shouted, 'we'll have to stop and fix that damn boiler again.' He thumped the taff rail with his fist. 'Damn it all.'

The Reverend Davies touched his shoulder. 'Don't fret, William. You've lost a little race,' he said. 'But you'll win the river itself in the long run.'

When the *Mary Ann* limped into Swan Hill at five that afternoon, the *Lady Augusta* was already receiving full honours on the river bank, having arrived some four hours earlier. Still, William struck his cap at a jaunty angle and affected an uncaring attitude as he displayed fine seamanship in coming alongside the bank and tying up opposite his much larger rival.

From the deck of his paddle steamer William could see a police station, a post office, an inn, a store and a dozen houses. Importantly, the town had a punt, making it an important thoroughfare for diggers on the way to the Victorian goldfields, explaining the many tents down along the banks and horses on the common.

'Rotten luck,' said Cadell to William with a smug grin, as they stepped ashore. 'You put up a good show.' He dropped his voice, 'though you might want to install a proper boiler.'

William was thinking what he would like to do with that boiler, for it involved a certain portion of his rival's arrogant anatomy, but he merely smiled and agreed.

The patronising applause, he, Tom, the two crewmen and the Reverend Davies received as they approached the tables around which the *Lady Augusta*'s company were arrayed, rankled more with William than the loss of the race itself. But he did his best and the company from the two ships ate together outdoors, catered for by the Inn's kitchens.

Governor Young himself sidled up to William later in the evening, but it was the Reverend Davies he was interested in.

'Dear Reverend,' he said. 'Would it be imposing on you too much to ask if, tomorrow being Sunday, you would celebrate divine service for us all?'

'Of course, Your Excellency,' said Davies. 'It would be my pleasure.'

At this Governor Young made a strange face, leaned forward and lowered his voice. 'Now I do understand that you are a Baptist minister, but I would count it a favour if you would read the Church of England service on this occasion.'

And the next morning, the full complement from both vessels, along with many of the locals, arranged themselves on the verandah of the inn just prior to nine am. William amused himself in recognising the various identities of the South Australian 'royalty.' The Governor of course, but also members of the Legislative Council: Grainger, Davenport and Younghusband. He recognised Kinloch, the clerk of the executive council, and the admittedly very beautiful Anne Finniss, wife of the Colonial Secretary, who shot William a poisonous look, as if to chastise him for being the upstart who had dared to challenge the mighty Cadell in his efforts to tame the Murray River.

The Reverend Davies, perhaps conscious that he would never again read a service for such a collection of dignitaries, celebrated the Church of England Liturgy with aplomb, albeit wearing a blue Jersey shirt instead of a cassock and clerical collar. As part of his sermon he read from Acts XVI: *on the Sabbath we went outside the city gate to the river, where we expected to find a place of prayer.* Overall, however, he kept things brief and to the point.

Afterwards, back on board the *Mary Ann*, William wrote a long letter to Bessie, enclosing a beautifully coloured feather from a parrot. The letter wasn't much, just a few thoughts that dripped from his heart, along his arm and into the ink of his quill.

> Tomorrow we will continue upriver, but the
> day will come soon, when we turn around
> and head for home. When the day comes
> that we land at Noa No, I will be on a fast
> horse and on my way to you with all
> possible speed.

He paused and thought carefully about the next sentence he would write.

> If I have learned one thing on this voyage,
> it is that living without you is impossible,
> and your mother's opposition is no longer
> enough to contain my growing feelings.

William sealed the letter in an envelope, ready for posting before he left Swan Hill the following day. The race against Cadell was all but forgotten. He had much more important things on his mind.

CHAPTER TWENTY-SEVEN

The Turning Point

AFTER SUPPER ON that Sunday evening, before the dancing started, Captain Cadell assembled his guests and crew on and around the promenade deck, with the tranquil warmth of the Swan Hill evening surrounding them. Anne Finniss listened in silence as the commander announced that the inaugural journey of the *Lady Augusta* would soon draw to a close.

'We have been part of a special trip – the first of its kind in the annals of this country. For just a few more days we will travel on upriver,' he said, 'to investigate the mouth of the Loddon, and then we must turn our nose for home. Our venture, however, is just the beginning of this grand vessel's history on the Murray. And soon there will be two, three, four sister ships, and the country's interior will awaken with the trading potential of this rich arterial river.'

While the applause carried on as it might for a well-received play in a city theatre, Anne thought to herself that there was a note of disappointment in the captain's tone.

She wondered if it wasn't now an urgent matter for Governor Young and others to return to their posts, Captain Cadell would have forged on upstream as far as it was possible to go. The fact that Randell was free to do so was an obvious humbug to the Scotsman, for he had been quite ill-tempered since the glory of winning the race had faded.

After Cadell's speech they tarried two more days in Swan Hill. There was a problem with the rudder, along with damage to the upper works from trees. The carpenter, Winsby and his mate McGregor assisted by other members of the crew and a few keen passengers, used this time to make repairs, and the sound of their saws, hammers, and workaday banter filled the steamer with a sense of industry. When all was ship-shape again, the fireboxes were fuelled and ignited and final preparations made.

Anne, ever since the night on which the commander had dismissed her from his cabin, had avoided his presence. But this did not stop her watching and trying to understand him. It seemed to her, when they steamed on from Swan Hill, that he wanted it made patently obvious that he was no longer in competition with the Randells. After so much speed and pace, he positively dawdled along these steeply winding sections of the river above Swan Hill, albeit dealing with winds just below gale-force.

For the first time since the trip began, Cadell was happy to stop the boat on any passenger's whim, and he laughed at any reminder of long and desperate night runs. He even joined in the frolics on the promenade deck and was, of course, an excellent dancer and much in demand.

In this mostly pleasant manner they reached the mouth of the Loddon – which was disappointingly narrow – for many of the passengers had opined that it would be a vital river route to the gold diggings, winding as it did almost all the way to Bendigo. Captain Cadell thoroughly charted the mouth area, then ordered a halt so his passengers could walk ashore on beautiful Wingieburt Island.

A few days further on, they dropped anchor at a station called Ganawarra. This heavily forested area was to be the zenith of their journey and there the *Lady Augusta* would remain for several days. For Anne it was a welcome rest from the voyage, and an opportunity to spend time with Travers.

Mother and son, along with most of the other passengers, visited with the station owners, in a fine homestead of adobe and thatch, on the banks of Gunbower Creek some two miles from the main river, transported there by ten fine horses in harness and saddle. They enjoyed the company of Mr Campbell, his wife, and his daughters. Each was more musical than the last, and they owned a piano. Anne, having sung once, was encouraged to do so many times, and she seemed to have found a new and thrilling timbre to her voice.

On the ensuing days Anne and Travers walked in wild scrublands, and she felt like a young girl again, able to delight in a butterfly, or a small dragon-lizard with its scaled back and gaping mouth. They skirted or paddled in limpid billabongs, sketched gum trees and reeds, while lorikeets and cockatoos whistled or squawked from the trees and vast flocks of water birds honked or rose into flight with the flapping of countless wings.

It was the strangest thing, but when Anne examined herself in the morning through the looking glass, she saw that her cheeks and nose had just the lightest scattering of freckles such as she had not displayed since her teenage years. It was as if youth was reclaiming her in those adventurous times.

Sometimes she and Travers walked with Lillie or Louisa Younghusband; occasionally with Mrs Irvine, but mostly just the two of them. Twice they saw Wamba Wamba people in their dugout canoes, poling between the reeds, calling out to the finely dressed woman and her son in their own dialect and the few words of English they knew.

The *Mary Ann*, which had been delayed by her own need for repairs, cruised past, heading upriver, and the guests told stories of the dark anger in Cadell's face when he saw the little steamer delve upstream. The Captain's jealousy of William Randell's carefree approach was becoming more obvious to Anne, and she began to see it as an ugly side to a man that she still admired.

All in all, these were beautiful days. In addition to walking, dining and collecting feathers or flowers, specimens of mica and chalk, Anne and Travers borrowed horses from the Campbells and went for a gallop to a set of low hills five miles from the homestead, looking across the river lands and together feeling goosebumps at the vastness of this country that they had been privileged to cross.

That evening, in a new spirit of closeness, Travers allowed Anne to read the journal he had kept of the voyage, and again her heart swelled with pride. His observations were so astute, his ear so sharp, that he had captured the spirit of the voyage. At just fourteen years he had the makings of a renaissance man – of letters, science and action all at once.

The next day Captain Cadell ordered all the company to board, and the *Lady Augusta* turned for home, with a stream of dark smoke from the stacks, and a slight wiggle of her stern as she settled into her course.

It was strange, but in those first couple of days, Anne realised that she did not think of Captain Cadell quite so much now, and even that she pitied him a little, for he bore the burden of his own pride like a hundred-weight of lead on his back.

Increasingly, over those days also, Anne was looking forward to seeing her husband and her other children again, very much indeed. She wanted with all her heart to be back in Adelaide, as a family, when this mighty adventure was done.

CHAPTER TWENTY-EIGHT

The *Mary Ann* upriver

OVER THE COMING DAYS, William Randell steered the imperfect but seemingly indestructible *Mary Ann* past the *Lady Augusta* at Ganawarra and further on upstream. The narrowing of the river from that point on was slow but noticeable, though there were good stands of timber on both sides, hence plenty of fuel, and there was no longer any competition to cause stress or provoke speeds that risked damage to the boiler.

Accompanied by the sounds of cockatoos in the trees, the Reverend Davies' singing, and the cycling of the engine, they forged on some two hundred river miles from Swan Hill. William would have loved to continue all the way to Albury, but not only were there reports that they would encounter a long, very narrow section of the river called the Barmah Choke, but their return home was overdue. They had been a long time away from the family, and most importantly in William's mind, the sight of his beloved Bessie.

They tarried only a short while at Hopwood's Ferry and steamed on to Maiden's Inn, the site of a small township that had been recently surveyed as Moama. The *Mary Ann's* reception at the inn there was so enthusiastic that it included not only the discharge of revolvers and rifles, but a small swivel gun.

This area was a hive of activity, being so close to the gold diggings: just fifty miles from Bendigo, one hundred from the Ovens, and thirty from the lesser fields on the Goulburn. The punt for which the area took its name was a large and robust affair on which William was surprised to see a full bullock team and dray being taken across, without the slightest stress on the part of the bullocky or ferryman.

The arrival at Maiden's Punt was a great moment for William, Tom and the crew, for here, at last, they were not overshadowed by Cadell and his official party, and were welcomed as the forerunners of a new age. The pioneers living in the area knew, from bitter experience, not so much the tyranny of distance, but the sheer inconvenience of it. River transport, powered by steam, was much quicker than draught animals on land, and the first Australian railway lines were still just sketches on a map.

After three satisfying days at Maiden's Inn, it was time to turn back, and as William farewelled an assembled crowd of well-wishers at the punt siding, he made a promise to return, not with just the *Mary Ann*, but a brace of paddle steamers that would keep station storerooms full, and carry the produce of the inland to market.

And as that game little steamer spun her paddle wheels and began to make way, William took a pinch of snuff and philosophised to Tom and the Reverend Davies. 'We won the race boys, we came further than Cadell and his pleasure cruise, and now we'll beat him back to Mannum.'

'No!' said Tom. 'No more races. Let's just do our own thing, brother, and let him do his.'

'Hear, hear,' said the Reverend Davies. 'Tom's right, William. Let's head for home, and don't spare a thought for Cadell if you can help it.'

'Of course, you're right,' William said. 'I agree. No more races.' He turned to the offing, a light river-scented breeze on his face, sounded the steam whistle once for the benefit of the farewell party, then pointed the bow for home. There was only one race he truly wished to win now, and that was into the arms of the young woman he loved.

CHAPTER TWENTY-NINE

The Downhill Run

TRAVELLING DOWNSTREAM, riding a capricious current, has proven to be dangerous. I have given orders to the officer of the watch that we should avoid the fast water where possible, but even so, at times we are gripped in the jaws of a rapid stream, losing steerage and sometimes spinning on our axis. Several times a day we pound into a snag or are carried under branches that scrape the upper works and cause consternation amongst the passengers.

Worse, the river has not stayed the same since our upriver journey. At one point we strike a newly fallen tree and rip open the side in a three-foot-long gash that has passengers screaming and men scrambling. Extricating ourselves takes an hour or more, and repairs to the damage much longer.

At the same time the river levels are dropping, and we run aground once, so severely that we end up resigning ourselves and stopping for the night. We are then forced to waste most of the coming day in drawing ourselves off the mud, using our longest cables and horses borrowed from a nearby station.

Yet, for all these alarums, we have the major advantage of requiring a great deal less fuel on the downhill run, and this saves time and labour as we stop to cut wood less often. My mind is focussed now on the making of money. At selected sheep stations on the outward voyage I made arrangements to collect wool on our return, to be carried at excellent rates. It remains to be seen if we and the *Eureka* can carry as many bales as we have undertaken to, yet every one we leave behind will be lost income – that William Randell in the *Mary Ann* will no doubt be happy to cram on board.

Downstream of Swan Hill we reunite with the *Eureka* and her crew, but this time we tow her astern rather than bear her alongside. Again, our journey takes us up the Wakool, sixty miles of the unknown, through the Stoney Crossing bar to Westmeath, where we take on wool – some two hundred bales. This is a cause for celebration – the first river-borne wool in the history of all the Australian colonies and provinces.

I insist that some of the ladies be the first to load a bale of wool, and the beautiful Anne Finniss (who still avoids my gaze), along with Lillie Younghusband and her mother do the honours, rolling the first of this piled-up fortune down over the bank and on board, to a chorus of cheers and shouts.

One very nimble crewman leaps atop the bale, just as

the lifting derrick on the *Eureka*'s mast swings it into the air. At some point high above the deck he waves his cap, and the stewards disburse a generous tot of grog to all hands at my orders, followed by the frothing, pouring, of champagne bottles in the saloon for our guests who lap the stuff up like pigs at the trough.

In the coming days and weeks we add to our burden of wool until both the *Eureka* and *Lady Augusta* are piled high with bales, stacked until the cargo resembles a ziggurat. It is all I can do to stop the children climbing like goats all over the carefully arranged commodity, in fear that one will break their neck in a fall.

When tragedy does strike, it is a man who falls victim, not a child. A Cornish stoker called William Teague is leaning against one of the gangway rails, filling a bucket of water, when the rail gives way. He tumbles into the water, and being unable to swim, splashes like a madman then sinks deep below the waters before the boat launched to rescue him can reach his position.

The run of bad luck continues, for as we steam on past the Murrumbidgee junction, the top-heavy nature of our load causes a problem. At Mr Grant's station we load six tons of wood he had cut for us, and soon after leaving, steaming towards Euston, the *Eureka* overbalances, swinging like a pendulum, and for a moment it seems that the vessel will founder. On the third swing, however, she rights herself, though some thirty-five bales of wool have fallen overboard.

We waste three hours recovering the sodden load, and as if to rub salt in the wound the *Mary Ann* returns from her sojourn upstream, heaving-to beside us. Randell has the cheek to offer to carry the offending bales for three pounds each. I wave him away, too angry to respond.

That night, with both paddle steamers anchored off the little town of Euston, the crews and passengers of both vessels are invited to the house of the Commissioner, a Mr Cole, for dinner and dancing, an invitation welcomed by our fun-loving circus-troupe of dignitaries.

I have much to attend to and arrive very late; after ten in the evening. I can tell by the looks of certain people that they have been talking about me; laughing at me. I burn with embarrassment, and make it my business to learn what the guests have been speaking of, and who has been making me the butt of their joke.

Once I have discerned this to my satisfaction, I approach William Randell on the verandah, where he is taking snuff and looking out at the river.

'How dare you!' says I.

'I beg your pardon?' Randell responds, yet I can see guilt writ large on his face.

'Why have you been telling all and sundry that half my cargo fell in the river?'

Randell chuckles, 'All and sundry? Who on earth would I be talking to that didn't already see it happen? Quite a few of the company here mentioned it, and why shouldn't they? It was just a mishap.'

'I'll thank you to keep your tongue still when it comes to my affairs.' I am near shaking with fury, though even I, in my heart of hearts know that my anger does not concern this one incident, but the knowledge that whatever the result of our race to Swan Hill, Randell is winning. I don't know exactly how he is doing it, but he is winning and I am losing.

'I think you are being overly sensitive about something about which there is no need to be.' Randell says, then slips his snuff box into his pocket and walks away, leaving me staring after him.

EPILOGUE

WILLIAM HAD VOWED that the first thing he would do on reaching home ground at Noa No was to catch a fast horse and ride it back to Gumeracha. It turned out that this was unnecessary, for Ebenezer brought a wagonette down with Elliot and their sister Elizabeth, with Bessie along for the ride.

On the way back up to the hills, with the horses walking steadily up front, William and Bessie sat on the load together, holding hands in the falling darkness, with familiar dusk river-country smells thick and enticing in the air. At first there were too many things to say, so much news to share, but by the time they had passed though the lantern-lit main street of Blumberg, William's mind had turned to weightier matters.

'I've been wondering, all these long weeks while I was away,' he said, 'if you'd like to marry me.'

Bessie threw her arms around his shoulders, and pressed her lips to his cheek. 'I've been thinking of nothing else all these long weeks. Of course I will.'

The matter, however, was far from settled. The following evening, back in Gumeracha, William set off across the street from his family home to Kenton Villa, with the purpose of asking Bessie's father for her hand. Taking his boots off at the door, he was admitted to the drawing room, with Bessie's siblings listening from behind corners and furniture, giggling and shooshing each other.

When he and the senior Nickels were settled in their chairs, William spoke out with his characteristic frankness. 'I have fallen in love with Bessie, and do believe that she feels the same way. I'd like to marry her, and I'm asking for your blessing.'

The blacksmith-heavy fingers of William Nickels tapped on the arm of the couch. 'Well, I suppose if Bessie …'

'You'd like fer to wed our Bessie?' crackled the voice of his wife, eyes stony and hard and her arms leaning like pillars on her knees. 'Never. We has already spoke on this matter an' I made me feelin's known. You, William Randell, be too old for a young gel, an' all wrapped up in that paddle steamer ridiculousness. The answer must be no.'

William looked back at her with a level gaze. He was a different man than he had been before he went away. Already a fit and strong young character, cutting fuel for the *Mary Ann*'s firebox had thickened his shoulders and fortified his arms with muscle. He had also learned something of the power of dreams combined with hard work. He was not cowed by Elizabeth Nickels, but was realist enough to know that he would not win by arguing against her, in her own home.

With a heavy heart, William walked outside to the garden, where Bessie was waiting to learn the answer. He led her away, and dried the tears that fell from her eyes with his thumb.

Life, unfortunately, is peppered with worse happenings than thwarted love. On the twentieth of December, just before Christmas, 1853, the Adelaide Times reported a tragedy. An article on page three carried the news that young Travers Finniss, son of the Colonial Secretary and his wife Anne Finniss, had been visiting with friends at a Mr Baker's station on the Murray a few days earlier when a 'melancholy and fatal' accident occurred.

With Mr Baker's two eldest sons, and another boy by the name of Nash, Travers had gone bathing in the river from a small boat. For reasons unknown Travers walked a short distance downstream, away from the others, to swim. A few minutes later, Baker and his sons heard a piercing cry. They rowed to the spot, shoulders burning with the effort.

Travers was nowhere to be seen. His mates, along with station workers, galvanised by shouts, dived repeatedly both in the immediate area and downstream. Many precious minutes had passed when an Aboriginal rouseabout found Travers six feet down, entwined with the reeds. He and two others brought the blue-tinged boy up to the bank, while onlookers wrung their hands and wept.

Mr Baker vainly tried to blow breath between Travers's lips, all the while praying for the miracle that didn't come. The boy was found to be deceased, and his body carried in a wagon to the home of his parents. There are no words that can pass through the years to convey how Anne Finniss felt on that day. No words can begin to describe the loss of her son.

Whether this tragedy was the catalyst for William's new determination to live his life the way he felt it needed to be lived we'll never know. But he was no longer a man to be thwarted. He had plans, and he wanted Bessie at his side while he pursued them. He managed to convince Gumeracha's Reverend Tuck that he and Bessie were meant to be together, without a parental blessing if necessary.

On the night of Christmas Eve 1853, Bessie waited until a little after midnight. By then the house was quiet, the last of the lights out. Her clothes were ready – a dress she had been secretly making with white charmeuse – purchased at the haberdashery in Kersbrook.

Out the window she climbed, face shiny with nervous sweat, carrying her dress and other clothing in a carpet bag. Walking on bare, silent feet, she headed out to the road where John, the second-eldest Randell brother, who had been co-opted as a conspirator, was waiting for her.

John smiled, 'Are you excited?'

'How can you ask? I'm beside myself.'

And in the house of the Reverend Tuck, Bessie retired to a bedroom to dress, before joining William in the drawing room, at which point she burst into tears with sheer joy. The Reverend waited until both she and William were calm enough to proceed. John was the sole witness, trying to hold back his own tears at the perfection of the union, and the long years of friendship that had preceded it.

Thus, in the early hours of Christmas Day, 1853, William and Bessie exchanged solemn vows and swore to be true to each other to their dying breath. With that they hurried out to a waiting trap that would take them away until the expected fury from Mrs Nickels died down.

Within a week they had become not just an inseparable pair, but an unstoppable force. Their honeymoon was, of course, conducted on one of the world's great rivers, steaming around quiet bends in the *Mary Ann,* walking river islands, and exploring hidden lagoons. Bessie was determined to learn the ropes, and William spent much of those days answering her questions, and showing her every aspect of steamer operation.

Over the years, Bessie spent as much time as possible on board, even when their children were very young. It was not unusual for the proud mother to take the wheel, with a blanket-swathed package in her arms.

In 1855 the *Mary Ann*'s hull became part of William's

new steamer *Gemini*, the second of many steamers in the Randell fleet. In following years William designed and built the *Bunyip*, *Bogan*, *Nil Desperandum* and *Ariel*. All were river icons, and a welcome sight from Mannum to Menindee, Bourke and Albury. They carried countless tons of wool, and desperately needed supplies into the interior.

For years William and Bessie ran this growing business from Wentworth, before moving back to Mannum where they built a stately residence overlooking the river, called Bleak House, in which they lived long and mostly happy lives.

The true father of the river trade, William entered parliament, and took charge of his late father's affairs in 1875. Even then he still operated paddle steamers, and climbed aboard himself whenever he could.

In the end, William Randell became the man that Cadell had wanted to be, a grand old man of the river, financially secure, with the respect of men and women from one end of the Murray to the other, the woman he loved at his side through thick and thin.

Captain Francis Cadell devoted the remainder of his youth to trying to develop the river trade, and to open up the many branches of the river. In 1854 he fell twenty miles short of reaching Albury in the *Lady Augusta*, and soon afterwards he had two new barges and two more steamers in operation.

Cadell almost perished in an expedition to explore the

Darling River anabranch, and by 1860 his business was in tatters and he turned to full-time exploring. Late in that decade, with growing debts, and contacts in high places disillusioned with him, he left the country.

Cadell liked attention, money and fame, and he went looking for these things in New Zealand, where the bitter Māori Wars were being fought. The Government welcomed the arrival of such an experienced man, appointing him commandant of the Waikato Steam Transport Service, with eight steamships in his fleet.

After the war, his attempts to make money became more desperate, and finally more cruel, as he turned to the slave trade known as blackbirding. He fell in with some of the most unscrupulous captains in the Western Pacific and Eastern Indian Oceans; men such as the notorious Bully Hayes. Cadell built slave barracoons on Barrow Island, off the Western Australian coast and filled them with tortured souls, plucked from their homelands to make him money.

Finally, he became the captain of a tramp steamer called the *Gem*. One evening, en route from Banda Island to Kai, a member of the crew, called Perman, entered his cabin. Cadell was lying on his bunk when Perman shot him six times in the body with a revolver. Later the killer told the rest of the crew that he killed his captain because he had paid no wages for five years.

In Cadell's last moments, did he remember Tenbury's curse from so long ago, when at the peak of his powers he raced with William Randell?

And the great river Murray, called Dhungala by the Yorta Yorta, and Millewa by the Ngarrindjeri, runs in good seasons, and stagnates in others. It has a soul but no conscience, and wears no chains. It rises and falls, and flows like the tears of a mother through eternity. It pauses for nothing, is majestic and ever-changing, bringing life to the outback through drought and flood, while the people of her banks come and go, as people have, since time began.

Acknowledgements

I'd like to thank the following people who assisted in the development of this story:

Murray River historian Frank Tucker who read a late draft of the manuscript and made hundreds of suggestions and corrections. Your work was invaluable. Any remaining errors are stylistic choices or last-minute mistakes and are purely my responsibility.

Noel McDonald who offered some valuable insights into the configuration and operation of the *Mary Ann*. Noel was part of a team (with Frank) who built a replica of the first paddle steamer on the Murray. Nic Klaassen for some pivotal research assistance. Nic is a South Australian history guru. Julie and Dean Olsen for welcoming my photographer and I to the amazing Randell's Mill in Gumeracha, now a bed and breakfast.

To the staff and volunteers of the Mannum museum, who have done such an amazing job of recreating the paddle-steamer era.

As always, thanks to my friends, family, readers and collaborators. You are appreciated.

More books by Greg Barron, all available at

ozbookstore.com, good bookshops, and Amazon's Kindle store.

Whistler's Bones

The story of Charlie Gaunt, who rode away from his Bendigo home and joined the famous Durack cattle drive from western Queensland to the Kimberley.

The Time of Thunder

In 1990 two men from across the world, linked by history, converge on Arnhem Land in a bid to solve the fifty-year-old disappearance of a man, and to uncover a Korean War mystery that will have global ramifications.

Camp Leichhardt

Ben Mulligan went down to the Roper River fishing camp to fish for barramundi and find peace. Instead, he found himself caught in a cruel conspiracy, and ultimately fighting for his life.

Outlaw: The Story of Joe Flick

Born in the battleground between two races, Joe Flick is a promising youth. A series of incidents lead him on a path that ends in a bloody tragedy in one of the most beautiful environments on earth.

Red Jack and the Ragged Thirteen

The Ragged Thirteen were a band of thirteen larrikins who put their stamp on Australian folklore with their devil-may-care journey across the wild Northern Australian frontier.

The Last Days of Dom Sebastian

Archaeologists Francis da Costa & Nicolá Massane follow
a trail of relics & myth, uncovering a tragic love story, and
a voyage past the edge of the known world to Australia's
Kimberley.

**Galloping Jones and other True Stories from
Australia's History**

Galloping Jones was a bare-knuckle-fighting larrikin who
could tame any horse. Moondyne Joe escaped prison
using an ingenious plan that made a whole colony laugh.
Based on the popular Stories of Oz history posts, these
sketches of Australia's past will inform and entertain you.
Above all, they will remind you of what life was like, in
the days before highways and smart phones.

All titles are available as eBooks and print copies are
always in stock at ozbookstore.com

Lightning Source UK Ltd.
Milton Keynes UK
UKHW041151190722
406064UK00001B/62